Liv

Also by Katie Campbell

fiction
What He Really Wants Is a Dog

poetry
Let Us Leave Them Believing

Katie Campbell

LIVE, IN THE FLESH

First published in Great Britain 1992
by Lime Tree
an imprint of the Octopus Publishing Group
Michelin House, 81 Fulham Road, London SW3 6RB

Distributed in Canada by
Octopus Publishing Group (Canada),
75 Clegg Road, Markham, Ontario L3R 9Y6

Chapter 2: Ties was commissioned
by BBC Radio 4 as part of
their 'Erotic Plays by Women' series.

A CIP catalogue record for this book
is available from the British Library
ISBN 0 413 45551 3

Phototypeset by Wilmaset Ltd, Wirral
Printed in Great Britain
by Clays Ltd, St Ives plc

For Michael

Some things can't be explained; they just are.
Love is transferable.
Location isn't actually everything.
People will surprise you.

Richard Ford, *The Sportswriter*

Contents

I Rivers

There are nine rivers flowing into the Thames, they say. Or maybe it is seven. The Fleet is only one of them, and now it is a road. It used to be where the newspapers were before they moved to the Isle of Dogs – so named because of the packs of wild dogs roaming its marshes. Or maybe it was originally called the Isle of Doges after some Italian prince who anchored there in the distant past. Elephant and Castle: the Infanta of Castile. History gets trapped in names. So flexible: explanations, speculations.

There are eleven bridges over the Thames in the City of London alone. The city of London is not the City of London. London, the city, is a sprawling mass of x million people and y square miles – there's no point in noting the figures here, the figures will change, the facts will remain; the trick is in the interpretation. The City of London is a single square mile in what is now the financial district, guarded at each of its four corners by a tiny grinning gryphon.

Gryphon: a fabulous creature with an eagle's head and a lion's body. Strong and vigilant/preying and ferocious. Often it represents Christ. Often it represents people who persecute Christ. You see the problem with interpretation . . .

Nonetheless, she loved reading guide books: facts, figures, explanations – they provide an illusion of control. Even if you forget the details, you remember the broader concepts: over half a dozen rivers flowing underground into the Thames. The Kil bourne, the Ty bourne, the Hol bourne, the West bourne: no wonder the city is so damp.

What else can one say about this person? She came from abroad, like the Infanta of Castile, like the Doge of the Isle of Dogs.

How does one sum up a life: thirty-three years? 'When Christ was my age. Or Mozart. Picasso . . .'

Let us begin again. Thirty-three years old with a halo of split ends. The colour bleeds from her hair like an old photograph. She lives in the clearing house of the world. When a woman is tired of London she can drown her sorrows a dozen times over without stepping into the same stream twice.

She likes to walk beside the rivers: the Thames, the Seine, the Danube, the Arno, the Tiber, the Hudson, the Charles, the St Lawrence, the Mississippi. Not The Mississippi, but a small Mississippi, named after the big one by a man who liked the sound of the word. An Indian word, chosen by a Scottish settler in Canada, naming a river which runs the length of a country he would never see.

All the mud-brown rivers which slither through the cities into the blood-red sea.

Red is the colour which leaks from her stories. Red is the colour of seals clubbed to death on ice floes, of whales harpooned in the ocean. Every living thing is under siege and several species die each day, hour, minute: who knows? She feels the human race should concern her more, but somehow the death of species seems more important.

But even that doesn't occupy her much.
And the human race hardly touches her thoughts.

The human race. It is the phrase which interests her. It fills her mind some days like the exercise wheel in a hamster's cage: the human race; the human race, the hum anrace, thehum anrace thehuman race theh uma nracethe hum anrace. Sometimes even less meaningful phrases fill her mind.

This is the trick: to chart the trivia, to capture the detritus which filters through the mind: grocery lists; polka-dots on a silk dress or a dog; the price of a piece of china; the flowers in a bouquet, the ribbons which bind it. Flashes from childhood: quotes, phrases. Words repeat, but once you try to write them down you lose them. In capturing things you transform them. Rivers are never the same. Can't be contained. Diverted, yes. Dammed up, perhaps; but even then they tend to retreat underground to bubble up later in some inconvenient place and time. London has seven underground rivers. Or is it nine?

Nothing here is made up. Nothing is entirely true. You tell a story once, you embellish it or edit for reasons of unity or economy, or artistic or poetic licence, or simply a lapse of memory. And suddenly the telling becomes the story and you've lost the real event.

Let me begin with a digression.
Let us begin with an aside.

Sometimes she counts in dentists' chairs. Sometimes she recites poetry remembered from her childhood – the year she gave up friends and memorized a poem a day, the year she gave up food and studied survival tactics in preparation for the apocalypse which only she believed in; the bleeding stopped, all the liquids dried up, she became small and hard as a stone, self-sufficient. Almost. Till the rains came and carried her away, burying her at the bottom of the river under the layers of rich brown silt.

Turning and turning in the widening gyre the falcon . . .
Things fall apart . . . The blood-dimmed tide . . .

Start again, that one seems to be buried for the moment.

I'll not oh carrion comfort despair . . .

She takes liberties with original texts. She adjusts the words for rhythm. Yeats and Hopkins wouldn't mind. If they did, there wasn't much they could do about it. Was there? Perhaps they were up there guiding the dentist's hand, inflicting greater or less pain as she got the words wrong or right.

Our father who are in heaven, Howerd be thy name . . . Howerd?

Dentists she didn't like. Doctors even less. Gynaecologists terrified her. Hands approach the gaping hole with instruments like lobster claws.

Once she'd been to a film with a man, a gynaecologist, although she didn't know it at the time. He just said he was a doctor; he didn't say he specialized. When the show was over they went for a meal. She wasn't hungry, she didn't want to eat, but she didn't want to seem ungrateful. This was a date, after all, and dates are hard to come by. 'Dates don't grow on trees you know.' In fact, they do – they grow on date trees in the desert. An emotional desert. Sometimes she feels like a desert. A dessert. A desert date for her date's dessert.

This particular evening she was feeling rather queasy, the film had been about pornography. They opted for Chinese: 'Anything that doesn't look like what it really is,' she said. She could eat anything if it was well enough disguised.

The man ordered crab. Whole, dressed crab. She watched, transfixed, as he twisted off each limb, snapped each joint, sucked out each length of shell till there was nothing left but the belly, the smooth, round, yielding belly of the crab. He stabbed it first with his fork, expecting some resistance, then when he found how soft it was he picked up his spoon and scooped out the flesh, slurping it up like soup from the bowl of its belly. That was the end of dinner for her. That evening, over coffee, he admitted that he was a gynae. Much to her surprise he stuck around for a while. Until she managed to prize him off. Salt helps on these occasions. Sprinkle a little on the offending body; it should shrivel up and fall away.

But this is not a love story.

I'm trying to sort out the contents.

I'm trying to split open the brain and release the seeds:

a golden shower – the god's gift to Danae after he raped her.

I keep getting stuck in the syrup, the sap.

Honey comes from the Greek word for saffron: a symbol of pure and divine light/an emblem of secular wealth and idolatry/a vulgar allusion to women's sex organs. 'I'd like to dip my spoon in her honey.' Etc.

Dearest J: I'm trying to tell you something. I want you to understand. Your two girls, they are the rings on the tree by which I count my years. My friend Anna is pregnant now. And R is still around. He gave me an antique pearl necklace to replace the one I lost years ago. Should I settle for him? Should I throw in the towel and try for once to create something that doesn't drift away?

How to anchor things? The knots between the pearls. The string gets grey so quickly; shall I have the pearls restrung? How to keep things with you? From what should we construct our lives, our stories of ourselves?

I dreamed I had a baby but it wouldn't suck from my breast. The baby was healthy, fine, the breast wasn't painful or swollen with milk; there really wasn't a problem except that it upset me that the baby wouldn't suck from me. I watered it with a watering can while weeding the garden each afternoon. This wasn't a malicious act; the baby blossomed in the sun. And my breast wasn't leaking, so perhaps it had no milk to offer anyway.

Goethe regarded the world as a greater genius than himself. He never created stories from scratch; no magician dealing in illusions, he drew from his experience. He milked his own life for his art. He fed his writing from the world around him.

Nothing is ever entirely wasted.

When I was a child we used to swim in the rivers where the logs came down. We were forbidden to swim in the logging season, but of course we did it anyway. Bobbing with logs, with trees, bobbing around in the river like the debris in the wide Sargasso Sea.

The trick was to grab a log and ride it a while, then shove off and find a new one to carry you further down with the current. There was always the danger that a log would hit your head, stun you, then the current would sweep you away and you'd drown. The more logs there were in the river the more dangerous it was. And exciting.

The rough outer bark provides a grip. But of course we all went for the slippery logs. That was the challenge, the game. The older logs that had been floating the longest were the most dangerous.

If they're left in the river long enough the water will consume the logs, breaking down their fibres, dissolving their structures till they sink to the bottom creating a thick, soft, rich, brown, muddy silt.

The rivers of my childhood were alive with dying bodies.

I shall always remember Picasso, a small man scurrying behind her brandishing his ineffectual parasol while she strides forward into the sun. The artist and his muse. He will never entirely overshadow her. There is some consolation in this.

Phrases, scraps of poems, an image: the woman with the spotted dog, the spotted woman with the dog, the spotted image of the woman with the dog. Numbers sometimes; sometimes just a word: nah nah nah over and over, like a headache you think it will never stop: nahnahnah filling every crevice of your head, stuffing it full like a cushion, blowing it up like a balloon expanding, the thin skin stretched taut till it bursts.

If you cough when they're taking an amniocentesis – think of it, you can watch it on the screen, the needle slowly entering the womb, the fatal point millimetres from the foetus innocently floating around like the ubiquitous cockroach in its own private pool, blissfully unaware of the lethal instrument poised at its heart.

It's all precision tactics: one jolt, one jerk, one wretching, wracking cough or sneeze or sniff and boom! The balloon bursts.
So much for that spot in the universe.
It's game over. One love. The foetus loses.
No return match for this baby.

I want to feel that weight, to hold that heaving, struggling body. Like trying to contain a river. How can you contain a river? How can you lead a child down to the water . . . ?

No, the child would twist from your grip, would struggle and scream and run away. Suffer the little children. Nobody would take a child . . .

No, it must have been a dream, a fantasy.

I long for somebody to call me Darling. I long to feel the edges of my body once again, to feel the edges dissolve and reform in somebody else.

Nothing is ever lost forever. Things simply get misplaced, misfiled. Everything turns up again, somewhere: bits of documents – a name, a phrase, a conversation – suddenly it appears on the screen. The machine misfunctions. Nothing is infallible. A life. A relationship. A body bobbing to the top, breaking the surface, shattering the mirror calm.

Where was I?
Words.
Yes. Sometimes they fill you to exploding.

2 Ties

They met at a lunch party given by an acquaintance. He was the last to arrive. The last person in is always an object of particular interest. He was the only one dressed in a suit and tie. Perhaps this made him seem important. Older. In control. Perhaps it simply made him stand out from the rest. Later she realized this was inadvertent; he hated drawing attention to himself. He liked to be discreet; he travelled incognito.

She was idling in a child's swing in the corner of the garden. He noticed her when the sun struck her hair. He strode across the lawn towards her.

When he stood beside her she felt a powerful physical rush. But it passed. It was pleasant, it pleased her, and it passed.

As they were the last to go he offered her a lift. They exchanged cards at the traffic light – she insisted on getting off at the tube, she wouldn't let him take her all the way. She was the sort who always went home on her own. He suggested they go to the theatre some night. She agreed, expecting never to see him again.

A few days later he rang. They met for a drink then went on to dinner. He asked if she had any children. No, she replied. She didn't explain. They talked about travel: when I was in Milan, Manhattan, Montreux . . . She didn't employ the unconscious pronoun of those who've been married for close to a decade.

After the meal they walked back to the car; she was driving this time. When she pulled up outside his place he invited her in for a drink, but she declined and drove off.

A few days after that he rang again. He was going off to a conference for a few days, could they meet up tomorrow and go to a film? Again she agreed, then cancelled on the morning, remembering a previous engagement, asking for a rain check.

A week later he rang again. He'd just returned from his conference, he was off for a fortnight's holiday, could they have that rain check tonight?

They went to a film she'd wanted to see but couldn't get anyone else to go to. It had been promoted as an arts film though at the end they both agreed it was a cheap excuse for soft-core s & m. Surprisingly, she didn't feel uncomfortable sitting beside him as the hero sneaked in and tied up the heroine. Even later, when the protagonists got to know each other and the heroine begged to be tied up, she didn't feel awkward with this virtual stranger sitting beside her. When it was over they both agreed it had been a lousy film and left it at that.

After the film they went on to dinner in Soho – a Chinese restaurant she'd often passed but never been inside. It was one of these places that look too authentic, too impenetrable, that look as though westerners would be committing some sort of indiscretion by presuming to enter. He said he had been taken there once by a Chinese friend. Something in the way he said it made her assume the friend was a woman. A business associate? she asked. He shook his head, but didn't volunteer any more information.

The menu was printed in Chinese with English translations in very small letters. She allowed him to order for them both, but declined his offer of saki or wine. When the food arrived it was all brown and black, all beans and entrails, not a green vegetable or a cashew nut in sight. It didn't taste bad though. It didn't taste like any Chinese food she'd ever eaten before, but in fact it was quite nice.

Later, when she drove him home and he invited her up for a drink, she answered, Why not? A quick one.

He offered her whisky, coffee, wine. She asked for a glass of orange juice. When he disappeared to get it she wandered round the flat assuring herself she could never live in a Victorian mansion block south of the river and certainly not one with grey-painted walls. He returned and sat down on the sofa, gesturing to her to sit beside him, placing his whisky glass beside her juice on the table in front of them. If you stand on tiptoes, he pointed out, you can see all the way to the Thames.

When she said she had to go he leaned across and kissed her quickly on the lips. I was hoping you'd stay, he said, without much conviction.

Perhaps I should stop the story here to point out that she realized later, when she was writing this down, she always knew a relationship was drawing to a close when she started trying to recall the beginning, trying to record the first and second and third conversations.

Whenever a relationship ends, you think: I'll never do this again, I'll never find someone else with whom I would want to do these things, to have this, this . . . intimacy. There will never be another person for me. And then there's the stage where you think: how do people do it? How is it done? How does one move from the furtive glances across a room to the sharing out of bodies? Baring souls is easy, it's the body that's the problem.

She hesitated a moment and he took the opportunity to put his arms around her. She froze. Then relaxed against his chest. You're unusually quiet, he said.

Hmm, she replied.

No questions? You're always so full of questions.

I find questions easier than conversation. Do you mind?

He shook his head. They fell into a pause during which he stroked her breasts lightly over her blouse.

After a while he asked her what she was thinking.

This is a false situation, she replied. I'm married.

Is your husband faithful to you?

That's not really the point.

Then why are you here now, with me?

He's away.
Is he away a lot?
She didn't reply.

After another pause he continued: do you love each other?

What does it mean, 'love'? she asked, knowing these were lines from a film/a book/a play – these lines, this conversation was a cliché; still she played it out.

What do you want? he asked.
I don't know.

She waited to see what he would say. When he didn't speak she continued.

If I were on holiday it would be all right, you know – with you and me. But since we both live in the same city . . .
Is he faithful? he asked again. Do you have good sex?
That's not the point either.

She waited: he didn't respond.

Sex is sex; we're a married couple. We've been married for a very long time.
I was married once, he muttered. On the night of the wedding I got very drunk.
Was it anger? she asked.
Not even that. I just realized it was a mistake. It was a rebound relationship. We never should have got together.

How long did it last? she asked, not that she really cared, she simply wanted to keep him talking.

My husband and I have been married ten years, she mused.
Maybe it will get better, he suggested.
She was surprised at the sympathy in his voice.
God, this is such a cliché already.
What?
Me talking to you about my marriage; you reassuring me.

A silence descended, which he broke by clearing his voice. If I had any say I'd try to persuade you to stay, he said.

If it were just sex I would take the chance; it's all the other stuff I don't want.

Like a little affection? he grinned.

No. Not that. It's the expectations and obligations and assumptions that it means something. It's the assumption of a future. I mean, if it's just a one-night-stand then it would be just that, a one-night-stand . . . She drifted off again before adding: and I'm not going to spend the night.

That makes it not adultery? he teased.

If you're prepared to accept it on those terms . . .

I'll take you as you come, he murmured.

The bedroom was dark, full of little boxes: leather and wood and tortoiseshell. A set of tarnished silver brushes lay face-down on the chest of drawers. The chest was mahogany: Victorian, perhaps late Georgian. It was heavy, large and masculine; it could have been attractive except that it sat on four short little legs. If it were hers, she thought, she'd cut off the legs. Of course that would destroy the unity of the piece, but on reflection – and she reflected on the chest frequently over the course of the relationship – she would sacrifice its long-term value for the immediate aesthetic relief. Sometimes she found herself feeling quite fond of the chest, squatting on its tiny legs like a fat old woman. Other times she despised it.

Sometimes, in the middle of the night, she would indulge in a slow, detailed fantasy of sawing off the legs. One by one. She could feel the shoulder-wrenching weight as she wrestled the chest over onto its side, the vibrations as it slammed on the floor, the sudden flash of lighter wood at the back where cheaper timber was used, where the wood was less worn by exposure, like a stretch of skin under bandages.

She could imagine the initial resistance of the wood as she drew the blade across its surface, the sudden acid smell of sap at the first bite of the saw's teeth. Then the aureole of sawdust framing the blade. Then the slow rhythm of the saw cutting through the legs, halfway through the rounded peg, three quarters of the way, till it snapped, till the leg came off in her hand.

She never told him how she felt about the chest. It was one of the few things they never discussed.

He gestured her into the room.
Would you like some water? He addressed the question to her back.
She nodded.
I suppose your place is much neater than this, he muttered, grabbing some clothes from a chair, throwing them into the darkness of an open cupboard, slamming the door shut before they could tumble out.

She didn't reply. She hadn't noticed the mess; she couldn't remember whether her bedroom was as messy or neat.
I have bottled water, he continued; would you like fizzy or still?

She listened as his footsteps retreated round a corner, through a door, off the carpet of the bedroom, onto the echoing wood of the hall. She heard the refrigerator creak, the hissing sigh of a new bottle being opened, the clink of ice being cracked into glasses then smothered with water.

She knew she should be exploring the room, gathering clues, but her mind was filled with the sound of his movements. A moment later he stepped up behind her. She turned and accepted the glass. She felt a ridiculous, self-conscious grin overtaking her. She took a drink, burying her face in the rim of the glass to hide her expression. It was fizzy; she'd forgotten it might be fizzy; she spluttered, coughed, spraying water everywhere.

Have you had many affairs? he smiled, searching in the top drawer of the chest for a handkerchief to dry her face.
A few, she replied, determined not to be fazed. Not many. No more than my husband has, I imagine.
But he had the first, she added quietly.

He led her from the threshold into the room.
Is that your wife? she asked as their eyes fell simultaneously on a framed photo beside the bed.

No. It's nobody.
She looks oriental.
She was a friend in Singapore.
You lived in Singapore? she asked.
It's just a photo I liked, he replied, turning it face down on the table.
I don't mind if she's there.
No, leave it, he said.
She hesitated a moment, then backed away.

Can we turn off the light? she asked. He had retreated to the corner of the room and was beginning to unbutton his shirt. He reached behind and flicked the wall switch. The room was still light from the streetlamp outside. She wanted to close the curtain, but she didn't want to be enclosed, alone with this stranger. She left the curtain and began unbuttoning her blouse.

Shall I get a condom? he asked. They were eyeing each other across the room.
Oh, yes. Thank you.
Would you not have asked if I hadn't said anything?
I'm at a phase in my cycle where I'm not likely to get pregnant.
Then shall I not bother?
I'd rather. If you don't mind. You always think that God is going to get you for the odd transgression.
I hope this isn't going to be an odd transgression, he replied.

Tell me your fantasies, he said.
They're pretty mundane really. I devise one and use it till it doesn't work anymore, then I construct another . . .
Do you have any particularly exotic fantasies? he persisted. No, it's better you don't tell me, or they won't work for you.

You talk so easily about sex.
She had never met a man who spoke so easily about these things.

When you've been through several long relationships you experiment.
Do you?
Don't you?

You learn to be easy about bodies when you live in a hot climate, he explained.
What climates?
When I lived in Mombasa . . . When I lived in Kashmir . . .
Why were you living in Kashmir?
When I lived in Jakarta . . .
What country is that?
. . . there was a whole quarter of the city where the transsexuals lived. You'd be driving along in the dusk, in the night, lit up by the braziers and gas lamps and the streets would be lined with these beautiful women flirting and joking in rustling silk dresses then suddenly one of them would lift up her skirts and they'd all squeal and shriek and laugh like drains and you'd see that they weren't really women, they were men, little shrunken men with these tiny little shrivelled up . . .

Singapore, Zagreb, Mombasa, Kashmir. He'd lived throughout the world. That was part of his appeal. For years she was convinced he was a spy, although he always denied it. She never actually lost the conviction, she just stopped caring after a while.

I think it's a generational thing, she said. You guys who lived through the sixties, you're easier about love and sex and talking; you guys who lived through the sixties . . .
And the fifties and the forties, he murmured.
Oh?
I was born on the first of May nineteen forty.

I was born on the fourth of May nineteen sixty-five, she replied.

So. We are both Taurus.

Once when they were making love *The Marriage of Figaro* came on the radio. He paused a moment as her opening aria drifted into the room.

What is it? she asked.

I once had an affair with a Suzanna. She was a Yugoslavian opera singer. Her husband was the conductor of the orchestra; we conducted our own little opera in the afternoons when he was rehearsing. Then in the evenings I would be there to hear her sing the pretty maid.

Suzanna, Donna Alvira, the Queen of the Night: there was a Mozart celebration in Zagreb that year. He didn't mention all the other parts. He let her believe it was a brief affair.

When were you born? she asked.

What difference does it make?

I just want to know.

Curiosity killed the cat.

Satisfaction brought her back.

Are you not satisfied? If you aren't satisfied, if there's anything you want me to do, just say, he said. She shivered.

I was born on the first of May nineteen sixty, she volunteered. No, nineteen fifty-five, she corrected herself. It was so long ago, I keep on forgetting, I keep on forgetting the exact year. I was born on the first of May, nineteen forty-eight, just after the war, she lied. No, May fifty-seven, I think it was.

So. We are both Taureans, he smiled.

What are the qualities of Taureans?

Stubborn, insecure, home-loving, artistic. Not risk-takers, he added, teasing.

Tell me your fantasies.

She hesitated a moment, then proceeded. I read a book once about James Bond – Ian Fleming. It suggested his mistress, Lady Somebody, had something over him. Some sexual thing . . . It hinted that she tied him up.

'Bond-age,' he grinned.

She could see him grinning down at her in the dark, in the light, in the shadow of light from the streetlamp outside.

I wondered, what's the appeal? she continued.

He didn't reply.

I suppose it's about power . . . She was talking to herself.

It's about relinquishing power; no, not simply power, it's about relinquishing control.

She could feel him breathing beside her. They were lying side by side staring up at the ceiling like an old married couple. She wondered if they were going to make love. He hadn't spoken in several minutes. She was trying to remember what his voice sounded like. She wondered if she had shocked him.

Then from the darkness beside her he spoke.

The instinctive response to pain – or pleasure perhaps – is to move away from it. When you're tied up you can't. That's the point of bondage. It enhances the pleasure.

Or pain, she muttered.

Would you like to try it?

She didn't reply.

This bed isn't very good for tying up, he added a few minutes later. But we could arrange something some time if you wanted.

And suddenly you find you're waiting for his calls.

– Hello?

– Hi.

– Hi.

Pause. What's there to say.

– Are you busy?
– I'm feeling a bit aimless actually.
Pause.
– It was nice last night.
– Yes.
– Shall we meet again?
– I'm going away Thursday.

(Your heart sinks, or his – depending on who's speaking. For once, why don't we say it's his.)

His heart sinks; you can hear it falling on the floor, rolling under the table to lie in the dust until somebody notices it there – the smell perhaps – the smell of rotting heart. Eventually it becomes overpowering, till someone bends down to investigate and sees the heart lying there amid the buttons and elastic bands and grit and dirt and long red hairs in their spider-web balls. So they sigh and groan and fetch the dustpan to sweep it away – the heart along with a brushload of dust.

– Can we meet next week? What about Tuesday? When are you free?
– Sure. Fine. Tuesday.
– Shall we meet Tuesday then?
– Yes, Tuesday.
– I'll call you that morning. Or you can call me. We'll arrange something on the day.
– All right. I won't disturb you any longer.
– You're not disturbing me.
Pause. Silence. Nothing more to say. There's never anything to say.
– So I'll see you Tuesday then?

And suddenly you find you're falling asleep. You know you have to go but you don't want to get out of the warm bed and walk down the cold hall. You don't want to go, though before you didn't want to stay. But you do go, if for no other reason than you said you would/you must/you couldn't stay. And even though he wants you to stay and you don't want to go, you do.

So I'll see you Tuesday then?

You think you've got it under control. You think it's a harmless, meaningless, light little thing.

Then the phone rings. You jump.

– Hello?
– Hi. It's me.
– I've been thinking about you.
– Snap.

Snap. It snaps. I snap, you snap.

At first you think it's all under control. A casual affair. A meaningless, harmless, casual affair. Then you find you're thinking about him. His smile; the crinkles round his eyes; the way he crooks his finger when he drinks his evening whisky. Evening, afternoon, first thing in the morning. You've never seen him first thing in the morning. You've never seen him through the night. Perhaps he drinks too much when you're not around to see him.

One of the things that amuses you is the way he suddenly jumps when he's falling asleep, like some little kid desperate to stay awake in case he misses something. You ask him about this one day, you say: did anyone ever tell you that you jump when you're falling off to sleep?

And he replies, nobody's ever told me before.

And you say, what is it? Why do you do it?

And he explains, I feel like I'm falling. Over the edge.

What edge?

An edge. Any edge. Think of it as a cliff if it helps you understand.

And suddenly in that tiny little exchange you realize that all this time you were feeling fond of him, feeling maternal, feeling he was like a little kid afraid to fall asleep, you should have been feeling concerned, that he was afraid to fall, that you weren't the only coward, that he was as frightened as you were, even more perhaps.

At first you think it's just a passing craze, and the way to get it over is to overdose, like honey or chocolate. As soon as one piece is finished you want another, so you take it. Again and again and again you go, in succession, waiting till you satisfy the craving. But you keep on taking, and the need doesn't diminish. It seems to grow. You find that you're not feeding the need, you're starving it somehow, somehow it's expanding. Like a balloon. Growing larger and larger. Until you're afraid . . .

And suddenly it isn't just the dull, indulgent craving; it isn't the sex, it isn't just the sex. It isn't the sex at all anymore. What you're looking forward to is the jokes and the giggles and the conversation and the stories and the anecdotes.

And suddenly it isn't just a passing fancy or a bit on the side or an adventure or an experience or lust or libido or boredom or obsession; it is, it is, it is that terrifying, that terrible, gripping crippling thing, that painful, that . . .

Suddenly you wonder, is this? Is this it? Is this The One?

How long has this been going on? Who is the man anyway?

You think it's insignificant.
You think it's just another thing.

Till you find yourself thinking about the tan line at the top of his thigh where his bathing trunks stopped in the summer. Or the way his little toe curls under the rest and wears away at his shoes. Or the streak of silver in his hair that you never noticed the first and second and third times you met.

How old is he? How old is he really?

But he's old enough to be her father! I mean who is this fellow? Who does he think he is, with his polka-dot handkerchief and his silk ties?

So you start going for long walks in the afternoon, after making love, then sometimes instead of making love. You pass a little estate agent's window: green shutters with pictures of houses set up in rows like a little toy village, all window boxes and white picket fences and views over the river. And you start to fantasize, at first in private, then as the fantasies become more real, more pressing, you ask each other, tentatively at first, not pressing, not demanding:

Tell me your fantasies.

No, don't feel you have to, then they might not work for you if you do.

But as the trust builds, or the need for bigger and better kicks grows, in the face of addiction to greater and even greater risks, you finally break down and tell:
  You tell me.
  No you tell me first.

And finally someone does.

Tell me your fantasy: the little doll's house, the white picket fence, the polka-dot dog in the flower-filled garden galloping down to the river. The champagne in the basket suspended under the balloon dangling over the water on a hot summer afternoon. Just the two of you, and the endless view and the champagne cooling on the ice, and the dog running polka-dotted below. And then you've reached a new stage, a different plateau.

Then you are hooked, bound, tied.
But what about . . . But what . . . But, but.

This is one of those stages where you replay the beginning to try to see how you got to where you are now:

– Can we cut the chat and the drinks and the lunch and the matinee stuff. I really haven't got the time and you can save yourself the money.

– I won't make any bones about it; I'm just here for the sex.

– I want this to be honest, to be a completely honest relationship. At least we can limit the damage that way . . .

(Can we limit the damage? Can we control it?)

– I'm not spending the night, you know.

'I'll take you as you come,' he replies.

(But you can't. You can't control it.)

– I'm a married woman, you point out; this is adultery, you know.

I'll take you as you come.

Where have you been? Where are you? Where is she?

She imagined the confession scene. She played it out in her mind every day, rehearsing the lines, devising her reply to every possible scenario. She worked out every possibility. She wasn't very good at improvisation; in fact it terrified her. It's the unpredictability. It's the loss of control. It's the fact that it's always the other guy who gets to write the lines.

I wanted to tell you a story . . . she began.

At first she wanted to tell it like a secret.
Guess what . . . A naughty secret to share with him.
Guess what . . . Then a coy, little, guilty giggle.

Or a confession:
Darling, do you have a minute . . . There's something we must discuss . . .

Or an anecdote.
Did I ever tell you about that man I met one Sunday lunch?

Or a story.
I once knew a man who said, when we were lying down in bed one time, the first time we slept together in fact, he said:

Tell me your fantasies . . .

The thing is, you can't . . .
You think you can keep it under control.
You think it is meaningless.
You think as long as you're honest you won't hurt anybody. Honesty. You cling to honesty and truth.

Tell me the truth, she said one afternoon. He was lying in bed waiting for her. He'd been waiting for an hour. The radio was on beside him: Radio 3 playing the *Enigma Variations*.

. . . No, please not that. Any other piece is all right. Not that music though. We played it at our wedding. Somebody gave us a tape; we took it on our honeymoon and played it every night . . .

The champagne was cooling in a bucket of ice on the floor beside the bed. He was reading a newspaper, in his polka-dot dressing gown with the silk cord knotted round it, smoking a Turkish cigarette, waiting for her. She'd been caught up in traffic – a funeral/a parade/a house-moving van – the cause didn't matter, what mattered was he'd been waiting for her. What mattered was she'd been delayed.

She had her own key. He listened for the sound of her key scraping in the lock of his front door. The sound of her breathing, panting: she'd been running up the street, up the stairs to his front door. She hurried down the hall. She stopped. She paused on the threshold of the bedroom. The sun bouncing off the polished floor behind her made a halo, made an aureole in which she seemed suspended.

Tell me, she said. Tell me the truth. I don't want to use you. Is this all right for you, just this, just sex? Because that's all I come here for. That's the only reason why I keep on coming back to you. I'm using you for sex. What are you getting out of it? What are you using me for? Are you getting enough? Because if you aren't, I understand. Just tell me. Just say it and I'll understand. I'll stop coming. She said. She said it once. At the very beginning. At the beginning of it all.

Who is the man anyway?! Who does he think he is?!

Darling, you're looking beautiful tonight.
  Why did you say that?
  I don't know. Because you are.
  There's something I have to tell you . . .

You think, as long as you're honest, as long as it's only you you're hurting, as long as nobody else knows, then where's the harm in it all?

How long has this been going on?

What are these marks on your wrist?

Most people use silk so it doesn't hurt so much when you twist against the cords, so they don't cut so deeply into your flesh. But it isn't really the binding that counts. In the beginning perhaps that's the thrill, but very soon the novelty wears off . . .

You know I couldn't live without you. Darling? Darling, did you hear me?

He's waiting.
He's waiting for you.
He's been lying in bed all afternoon waiting for you to come and release him.
He's falling off the top of a bridge.
He's standing at the edge of the sea and you're the only one who can save him.

Where have you been?

Of course if we were on holiday in some exotic place it would be all right. It would be easy. It would be meaningless. But this is real life, so we can't go on.

Don't you have any dreams? Don't you have any fantasies? Tell me your fantasies.

The real thrill, the terror, is the possibility . . .

It's the idea of response without responsibility. It's relinquishing control, like a child, like a lover, like a dying man sliding off a cross. Like the balloon floating over the river, higher and higher, till the houses look like polka-dots and the cities look like handkerchiefs and the river looks like a long silk cord snaking over a dressing gown.

The very real, though distant possibility . . .

Darling, did you hear me? Where have you been? You know I would die, I would fall down and die, I would jump into the river and drown myself if you ever were to leave me.

. . . That you will never be released.

3 Derb

Away. I've gone abroad again. This urge to move, to travel, to be anywhere but where one is. Some things you carry with you. Transformed, transmuted, like the underground rivers which rise up unexpectedly, flooding the commons, creating havoc miles away from where you thought you left them.

What does it mean when a body misfunctions? A cancer, a miscarriage, even a pregnancy perhaps if it's unplanned and unwanted?

The slow disintegration. Losing one's grip.

Pain.
I lie here dying.
To move is agony; to remain still is worse.
I can't endure it. Daggers jousting in my gut? my side? my belly? I can't even locate the pain; it's spread in a band from my thighs to my chest.

The vomiting begins.
It brings no relief.
Every half an hour.
Now it's a ball of agony in my side, but each rush to the sink leaves it undiminished.
I've thrown up supper and lunch and breakfast and there's nothing left inside, but I keep on heaving.
Loud, wracking waves of vomit, like some donkey braying: wretch, wretch, wretch, wretch . . . down to a whimper.

The noise echoes round the courtyard, intimate and obscene. Everyone must hear it: all through the quarter. The obscenity is multiplied, in this Arab culture, in this house of men, in this season of Ramadan.

This isn't a story, it's an episode. It does have a beginning, and a middle, and an end – of sorts – but the parts merge into each other.

It began when I was driving back through the Atlas Mountains with Oliver. My bi-annual sibling visit. Late April. We had been to the desert. The ride out had been in fog, but when it lifted I saw exquisite poppy fields and donkeys with panniers heavy with daisies and flower-studded grass. I was hoping we'd see the fields on the way back but as soon as we left Ouarzazate and started climbing the storm began. Rain, hail, snow, the hairpin turns, the road crumbling beside us, the Volvos looming out of nowhere . . . At least the Berbers weren't chasing the car, trying to sell us their lapis and silver.

I first felt the knot in my side as we came through the high pass; I knew then that we were on the last lap, the top of the mountain. I thought it was nerves, so I didn't pay much attention.

Back at sea level it was glorious, sunny, everyone cycling through the eucalyptus-lined evening streets to break the fast. Although it was almost May there were still some oranges left at the top of Oliver's trees. The parrot screamed and the doves cooed as we entered, like pilgrims from a distant land.

We ate lobsters that night – a gift from a friend who'd come from Essaouira. Then we sat in Oliver's study with the windows open onto the courtyard, and the fountain trickling, and the CD playing the 'Nimrod' piece from the *Enigma Variations*. In the square the Ramadan songs blared from the loudspeaker. Next door an Arab man was singing. From somewhere behind the kitchen came the sound of the kitchen boy's TV. I thought, perhaps I could live here; perhaps I could simply stay here forever, never go home again.

I looked through the *Herald Tribunes* from the previous week, then we said goodnight. I was due to leave the next afternoon. My husband had agreed to pick me up at Heathrow in the evening. I planned to spend the morning in the souk buying trinkets to take home. I'd seen a dark blue lapis ring: a peace offering for my husband, a thank you for picking me up at the airport. If he did. If he didn't show I would give it to R, even though I've told him that this thing, this affair between us must end.

I've given up turning on the light, some crazy notion of not waking the household. Anyway, I know the route from the bed: three steps through the bathroom door, two more steps to the sink. Toward morning I see it is black that I am throwing up. Blood? Every sip of water causes a new stream of vomiting. Now there is the thirst as well as the pain.

Dawn begins: the parrot, the cacophony of birds. The alarm announcing the fast has begun: tinny, sinister, it begins with a rising siren. No gentle reminder this – it is exhorting, it is threatening, a hellfire-and-damnation threat. It all seems to mock me through the pain. A dying pain. A dear-God-let-me-die-I-can't-stand-anymore-of-this pain.

When it is light Oliver knocks on the door bringing me dramamine and a sleeping pill. I promptly throw up both of them. He says he'll look for a doctor as soon as it's morning. He looks doubtful. It's a bad time to look for doctors. People are supposed to be praying to Allah, contemplating their sins.

Poor Oliver, his life is so calm and ordered and free from disruptions. He hadn't bargained for this dragging dependency, this terrible debt of family. That's why people move to Morocco – to get away from this sort of thing.

It must be morning. Wednesday. It being Ramadan, or perhaps simply it being Morocco, the doctors don't answer their telephones. The hours pass. They must be passing. The sink isn't draining anymore. I can't bring myself to throw up in the can. Habib takes his moped to a French doctor he's heard of. The doctor agrees to see me. It is four o'clock. Afternoon. The doctor will have to come here. I can't get up.

I'm going to die. I want to die. Oliver and Habib carry me through the alley to a place wide enough to bring the car.

Today I'm supposed to be flying home. This will pass. Somehow. Either I will die or I will live. I don't believe in death, I don't think. Soon I will be preparing to leave, sitting on Oliver's terrace, lying in my own bed in London. My bed? Our bed? In truth I think it belongs to my husband. I suppose I will leave it with him when I go. If. But now there is simply this pain which must just be endured. I long for a deep, cathartic cough, for something to drink. A cold glass of water.

I'm wrapped in a heavy, orange cloak. Beautiful braiding. I'm afraid I'll throw up over it. Oliver brought along a basin. It smells of soup. The smell makes me sick. I try to push it away. The city is endless. We drive for hours.

The waiting room is dark, dingy. Several robed women are eyeing me warily. Habib leads me to a little side room with a single bed. I lie there. We wait.

The doctor arrives. Attractive. Calm.

The doctor directs Oliver and Habib into another room. He motions me onto the table. He examines me. He orders a blood test. If the count is 7,000 I'm all right; if it's 10,000 I can travel tomorrow; if it's 12,000 he'll have to operate. I forget to ask what they're counting, what the operation will be. He gives Oliver the address of the lab and a prescription to stop the vomiting.

We trail back through the waiting room. A man waits there now. He looks disapproving. I'm an intruder in this culture; a white woman, dragging her illness, parading it in this flagrant manner.

The blood test. Oliver goes next door to fill the prescription. Habib holds my hand. The needle is huge. I shudder, recoil. The pharmacist jokes that children aren't afraid of it. I reply that I am not a child. I drink the prescription on the steps. I'm not allowed more than two sips of water. I sneak almost the whole glass before Habib takes it away. Orange juice. Fresh-squeezed orange juice with ice; I would die for it.
We wait on the steps for the results.
The blood count comes through: 25,000.

The doctor rushes me into a clinic. Oliver goes to collect my things. He hates illness. It runs in the family, this fear, this incapacity in the face of illness. It touches me to see it in him. Habib remains with me, talking to the technicians, joking with the nurses, translating their Arab into French for me. I feel more comfortable with him than with Oliver. Although he is Arab and not family, at least he is my age.

'Take off your shirt,' the technician directs me. Habib turns away. Does he have sisters?

The technician jams my chest between two plates. Do they know that X-rays cause cancer?

Hospital nightgown.
A tiny, windowless room.
A high, narrow bed.
A shower, sink, a telephone with no numbers on it. No facecloth or towel or soap. No hot water.
I'm hooked to an IV which should lessen the thirst. It doesn't.
The pre-med. The pain.

A girl comes in. Habib steps out. She shaves me with a blunt razor and a bottle of iodine.
Is this necessary? I ask.

It is.
Why?
'Il faut avoir un champ net' – a clean field. The battle continues. Allah's revenge on the fair race. God's punishment perhaps for my affair with R: all the lies, the deception. All the pain we inflict upon each other.

I watch the veneer of adult sexuality slowly scraped away. The childish shape emerges. I am powerless. Habib returns.

My doctor enters in a leather jacket. He tells me the operation has been delayed because a baby is being born.

My hair is caught up in a cap. The girl wheels me down the hall. In the operating room is a man I haven't seen before. He doesn't speak to me. I want my French doctor. I don't want this stranger touching my body. He puts the anaesthetic into the IV, a thick, clear liquid: Lethe, River of Oblivion.

I try to keep him talking. I ask if it will hurt, if there will be a scar. I know I'm not making any sense. I know he's humouring me till I fall asleep, but if I keep him talking long enough perhaps my doctor will return.

Nah nah nah. I'll not oh carrion comfort . . .

I wake up in 'reanimation' – recovery. My arms are strapped down. Tied. Fever. Thermometers. Pain. People pass through but nobody stays. The nurses stare at my fair skin. Someone bathes my face. They wheel me back into my room. There is a radio beside the bed, tuned to the BBC. The nurse explains that Habib brought it.

Oliver comes. He rang my husband. They get on well, he and my husband; they're both of an age. A grey, friendly, age. They understand the value of politeness. They exchange comments across the newspaper. My husband likes the taint of Bohemia; he often mentions that his brother-in-law lives in Morocco. I wonder why he hasn't telephoned me here at the hospital.

I lift up my gown. I'd forgotten they shaved me. I look like a bald, little, naked mouse. Above the mound, inches away, is a large, white bandage. That's where the appendix was.

Why? Why me? Why now?

'These things just happen.'

An obsolete organ suddenly bursts into life, festering, poison, threatening explosion.

Sleep. Pain. Beginnings of boredom. A jab. The fifth or sixth of the day. My thigh is bruised from the jabs. Sleeping jabs, painkilling jabs. They seem to do it with blunt needles. Do they sterilize the thermometers? Do they know about AIDS?

Today is Friday. It happened on Wednesday – Tuesday night. The nurses are nice, but very slow. One left a thermometer inside me for thirty-five minutes. Another time I asked for a bed-pan. They left it under me for hours. These small humiliations. I struggled to remove it. I put it on my bedside table. Two doctors, three nurses visited, but everyone ignored it. Finally I called a nurse to remove it. She put it in the bathroom. Later I saw it there, still full. The next morning I tried to empty it; I couldn't lift it without ripping my guts open. Gutted. I like that word. I suppose somebody did, eventually, empty the bed-pan.

I ask for water, a towel. '*Oui, Coco.*' The older nurse calls me that: '*Ça va, Coco?*' They think I'm sweet. I tell them I'm thirty-three years old. They don't believe it. New nurses come in and ask me my age, to make sure they've heard correctly, or that I've understood the question.

'And where are your children?'

They don't believe I have no children.

'And have you a husband?'

Sort of. It's too complicated to explain. I say I have. Now they disapprove. Married, middle-aged and no children. The younger ones lost interest when they heard I wasn't seventeen.

The desire to cough. Terrible pain.

Habib brings Fatima to visit on his moped. She's all dressed up in a blue and white synthetic jellaba. Her face is veiled. When she cleans the house she wears trousers, like me. The veil is like a hat - a gesture of formality. I wonder why he's brought her. To counteract the intimacy of having seen me almost naked?

We sit, Habib and I talking in French, Fatima smiling. She has brought me a present, a postcard, a picture of Morocco. She pronounces the word 'Picasso', and grins. She's been practising the word all morning. The postcard is of a painting by Matisse. I smile and nod and repeat 'Picasso' with her.

Yoghurt and apple compote. The drip is removed. The arm feels like a pincushion. The yoghurt smells vile. As do the anemones Oliver brought. A foetid smell. I want to remove them but I don't want to hurt his feelings. Habib leaves. Fatima stays. I try to talk to her in French. I wonder if it's my accent or if she doesn't speak the language. Oliver addresses her in Arabic. She points to a pile of folded clothes. Habib took them home that first night; she's brought them back, washed and ironed. A few minutes later she goes. Why did she stay on? What did she want from me, knowing we had no language in common? Perhaps it was simply a gesture of friendship. Woman to woman, cutting through cultures, generations.

Oliver will be coming in soon. He walks from the Derb. Derb means alley, dead-end really. Oliver lives on a dead-end. It takes him three quarters of an hour to walk to the hospital. He could drive, but the streets are crowded during Ramadan. People are crazy, they wander back and forth in front of cars. Besides, he says, he likes the exercise. He walks in, then he sits with me for ten minutes, then he walks home. On the way he stops for a beer with his friends at the top of the Hôtel du Boulevard. Usually they meet in a local café, but during Ramadan the local places don't serve alcohol.

Sometimes he returns in the evening for another short visit.

I make a point of hobbling past the nurses so they can see I'm getting on. I clutch my gut, hunched over. It feels as though my stomach will spill out if I stand up straight. The old nurse clucks approvingly. The young nurses ignore me. One of them, taking my pulse this morning, asked if I had any make-up. Perhaps she wanted to steal it. She flounced off when I said I didn't use the stuff.

All the phone lines to Morocco are down. That must be why my husband hasn't telephoned. Oliver arrives very late and harassed; the queues at the Air Maroc office were endless because all the computers were down. The doctor has said I can fly in a few days.

My husband rings. When he finally gets through he is angry, upset, worried. He offers to come out and get me. He always comes through in response to an illness. I burst into tears. It isn't the pain. It is . . . what? An audience. And knowing that it's such a long way home.

He asks where Oliver is. He's having a drink or dispatching a story or doing whatever he does in the day. My husband is surprised that Oliver isn't with me. In his family everything stops for illness, everything revolves around, adjusts to, illness. He can't understand our attitude: that illness is an embarrassment; that one mustn't indulge the patient; that the patient mustn't increase the disruption by expecting any favours.

This is perhaps why I cry: because if he were here he'd be with me, no matter how bad things are between us, no matter how much anger and pain. He wants to come, but I dissuade him. I haven't told him yet that I didn't take out insurance. I can't think where we'll find the money. We. I assume it's still we – I assume both partners are liable for the bills if they aren't yet divorced. Oliver says he can cover the expense till I pay him back, but I know he can't. He gets by, writing his pieces: travel books, features, the odd news dispatch. It's a living, but not enough to accommodate the emergency appendectomy of a barely-known half-sister.

The evenings are endless. Pain versus boredom. Boredom is what I dread most of all. In life, in death. The room smells of camel. Is it the clean laundry Fatima brought? The soap? Or me? Or my nightgown? I can't locate the smell but it sickens me. The hospital gets busy at dusk with everybody having their supper as soon as the fast is finished. There is another flurry at ten when all the visitors leave. Then it's silent. The night-nurse – a great motherly figure – comes in: *'Tu as bien mangé?'* I explain that I haven't been given anything to eat since noon. She bustles away and returns with the ubiquitous compote and yoghurt.

All last night a man cried in Arabic. Singing? Preaching? Wailing in pain? This morning they offer me a painkiller, but I think the pain of the needle is worse than the pain it's designed to kill.

Saturday. Boredom. Biscotti for breakfast. Food is a major preoccupation. What did you have for lunch?

Supper? What's the weather like outside? They changed my dressing today. I've stopped having the needles. Now they give me huge capsules to swallow after every meal.

Poor Oliver. He didn't bargain for this intimacy. I asked him once if he thought our father was a happy man. It's not the sort of conversation that interests him. 'As happy as anyone,' he replied after a long pause.

Terrible headache. Too much reading. The doctor examined the stitches this morning: seven ugly insects crawling across my abdomen. I hadn't thought about the scar. He says I can go tomorrow morning. I burst into tears.

Why not tonight? You said I'm healing impeccably.

He smiles: 'It's best to be sure.' Then he disappears.

It takes me fifteen minutes to struggle out of bed, another fifteen to make the three short steps to the bathroom. The exertion of this journey exhausts me. One's horizons narrow. I washed myself this morning. Lunch arrives: a bowl of soup. Vetiver tea three times a day.

Sunday morning. The luxury of being able to cough, or to sneeze, or to climb out of bed. Last night I read till midnight. The night-nurse hovered.

'Ça va?'

Oui, merci.

'Mieux?'

'Oui, beaucoup mieux . . .'

She was relieved when I finally turned out the light.

A woman is shouting down the hall. The nurses laugh. The place is staffed by women except for the two doctors – my French surgeon and the Arab anaesthetist. I think the girls with the pink hats are the lowest. They change the beds and gossip in Arabic. The older women with the white hats take my pulse and tell me what I can eat. Then there's a severe woman in a turquoise fez who follows two steps behind the doctor; nobody jokes when she's around.

This morning I'm allowed to go. Up, washed, all my things waiting. Where is Oliver? I'm wearing the trousers and sweater I huddled in here four days ago. Only four days. I'll melt in this heat. Waiting. My arm still aches where the IV was. It's left a little, round, red hole.

The body becomes a separate thing, a machine, an instrument connected through pain. I stand back from it – this thing which failed me. This feels like the beginning of chaos. I used to think I was in control: of my body, if not of my mind.

They give me the appendix in a little glass jar. It looks like some bit of octopus you'd find in a cheap Greek stew. I want to throw it out. I suppose I should take it back to England. I read that the appendix is the end of the intestine. It used to be a second stomach. Over the millennia it has atrophied. Usually it just lies there doing nothing till you die.

Finally Oliver arrives. A beautiful morning. The sunlight. The Atlas Mountains rise all snowcapped, all exquisite and exotic, all pure and unassailable, defining the horizon, miles and miles away as we drive past the old mosque, the souk.

The roads are full of donkey carts, heavy with onions and oranges. Terrible, thin, bony donkeys driven by terrible, thin, bony men. Bridles of twine scrape the animals' faces. Oliver drives as close as he can to the Derb, easing between the crowds and the bikes and the donkeys and the people sitting on the ground selling pots and bundles of mint and second-hand drugs and dusty jewellery. We pass a dead dog by the side of the road. Oliver glances up to see if I've noticed. I look away, pretending I haven't.

You can't take the car right into the quarter, the streets are too narrow. There are always the last few alleys to negotiate on foot. The dirt seems oppressive: the stench, the horse-shit, and dog-shit and cat-shit and piles of rubbish rotting in corners under the darkness of the arches. Before it seemed so quaint. Something has changed.

Oliver opens the low wooden door into his courtyard: roses, palms, orange trees, freesia. And the fountain. And the cages of birds all around the walls. And the wild birds in the trees. And the pain suddenly lifts.

Fatima rushes to greet us, then steps back politely. Such dignity. She has been working for Oliver since he moved to the city twenty-five years ago. She has one daughter and two sons, both in the army. The third son, also a soldier, was killed in the Algerian war. Fatima's husband left her years ago. In Morocco a father is financially responsible for his children, but it's difficult to enforce the law, especially if the man is in the government, which he is.

Monday: I'm sitting on the roof terrace, between the palm trees and the jasmine.
That first afternoon I knew I'd be here.

Oliver bustles around me. The sun is so hot that he can make jam by mixing berries in a sugar syrup, then leaving them in a bowl on the roof with a piece of glass over the top. The heat causes condensation, so the jam thickens without the fruit losing its shape. He pours off the condensation several times a day. In twenty-four hours he has five jars of perfect strawberry jam.

Fatima's daughter came by this afternoon. I was sitting in Oliver's study. The kitchen boy led her into the room.

She spoke to me in French. She sometimes helps Fatima with the cleaning. She's twenty-one and lives at home and doesn't have a job because of the unemployment. She'd like to be a hairdresser. She'd like, even more, to be married. She's been asked, but she didn't like the man. What she really wants is children. Did I have children? No. Did I want children? Yes. Perhaps. When the time was right. She looked at me sympathetically. She wore a synthetic jellaba. Wasn't it hot? It was. Usually she wore clothes like mine. I suppose she dressed up to visit me. We ran out of things to say. Finally she left. Perhaps Fatima was afraid I'd be lonely. Perhaps Oliver asked Fatima to ask her daughter to visit me.

Tuesday: 'Arouda, Arouda,' a constant cry throughout the day. Arouda is the kitchen boy. Oliver says he's stupid and a liar. He hangs his head in a permanent gesture of apology. 'Aarouuuda': the name is full of remorse. Arouda left the door unlocked so the moped was stolen. Arouda forgot to feed the parrot so it died. Arouda left the iron on and burned a hole in the bed sheet . . . Arouda forgot to walk the dog . . . 'Arouda, Arouda, Arouda.' The call blends in with the dog's panting and the cooing of the doves.

Fatima's daughter comes again. She is dressed in bell-bottomed trousers. She asks how I am, and whether it hurt, and how long I was in hospital. Fatima comes through and scolds her. The girl rises to go. As she is leaving she turns and asks if she can see my scar. That's what she's wanted all along. I lift up my shirt to show her. There's nothing to see but the bandage. She is clearly disappointed. All that fuss for a little bandage. She shrugs and disappears.

Wednesday: yesterday evening I went back to the hospital. The nurse changed my bandage, the doctor examined the stitches and said I could travel. He shook my hand and said again that I was impeccable.

Oliver took me to the airport this morning. He had a wheelchair waiting in the parking lot. He wheeled me past the guards with their machine guns, through the queues of tourists. Everyone stared, as though I couldn't see them looking. Oliver sat with me till the flight was called, then he found a stewardess to wheel me through. Now he's disappearing through the glass doors of this tiny airport.

In four hours my husband will pick me up at Heathrow with another wheelchair. He will be concerned, considerate. And all the major decisions will be put off for a few more weeks or months, but eventually we'll have to confront them.

This, I suppose, is where the story ends – no, the episode.

On the first night of the pain I thought I wanted to die, I thought: this is the worst ordeal of my life. But even as I thought it I knew it would end, one way or another. And that second night, in hospital, when the pain alternated with despair, I knew this moment would come; the moment when it would all be over, when life would close over the unforeseen gap and continue on, and soon the episode would be an anecdote, then a recollection, then it would fade and almost disappear, like the scar on my belly will do. It won't disappear, but someday I'll look in the mirror and I won't even notice it.

4 Lifts

You shuffle in. The door closes. You anticipate the fall. It doesn't happen. The door opens. Eyes gaze intently up at the ceiling, down at the floor. It's too heavy, somebody mutters. Nobody moves. A crowd is waiting but there is no room. The door rattles closed. You anticipate . . . what?

A moment. A pause. It jerks into action. The slow descent. The sudden stop. Bodies thrown against one another. It opens. People slip away: the human streams, the underground rivers. Nobody merges with anyone else.

Waiting at the airport. People pushing recalcitrant carts along the barrier. Looking hopeful, looking anxious, trying to hide their fear with that smile which freezes: nobody is in the sea of faces lapping at the finger-smudged glass. Then the burst of relief when they finally find the one who's waiting there for them.

Waiting. Watching the faces. Wondering if you'll recognize . . . The black hair has turned white, the copper has turned grey. The lines . . . People age so! You hide your shock in a wide embrace, laughing. Laughter leads to laugh-lines. Frown-lines. Lines which frame the mouth and eyes like rays from a child's beaming crayoned sun, slowly burning itself to extinction.

Matching the faces. Old men greet young girls: fathers, lovers, kindly uncles whose fingers probed in private places long ago and now forgotten. Some rush and hug with an equal exuberance. Some slap each other, embarrassed but affectionate. Some tentatively offer a cheek to be pecked or a hand to be shaken.

And then there are the mysterious ones, the people met by drivers, the cold welcome of a chauffeur's cap, a hand-printed card proclaiming the name. Do they envy the chaos of flesh or have they chosen their own solitude? Could I love this one or that one? Could I be the person who waits for him?

What of the ones who travel with luggage wrapped in brown paper and masking tape? Or the ones who travel with matched leather suites? Or with fraying backpacks? Or with canvas bags and expensive-but-sensible walking shoes? I could be that woman. Could I? Is she any happier than me?

The 'Darling, where were you's as the crowds disperse and the anxious stragglers finally unite until there's only one old woman left on the bench waiting for tomorrow and tomorrow, grateful for a place to sit.

This woman muttering alone; her story is so plausible. How easy to cut loose and drift away, to end up muttering in the crowd. Dear God . . . Dear Mum . . . The prospect terrifies. Is this the point of couples, of families, community: this weighing-down, this anchoring?

Am I learning all of this too late?

In Romania a woman broke down. It was reported in the newspapers that Christmas that it all collapsed. Describing the lynching of a Securitate squad on the street outside her window she explained that when their cars were set alight – twenty gas tanks blazing an arm's length away – she realized that that was the first time it had ever been warm inside her apartment.

. . . The smell of charcoaled human flesh still lingers in her furniture.

You get in the lift.
It's just you and another man.
You look, he looks, a barely perceptible nod, then both of you gaze at a spot on the floor.

The cage vibrates a moment then hums. Then shudders. Halts. You hang there, suspended, you and the man.

The door doesn't open. You've stopped just short of the top.

Eventually you confront him. You look the man in the face, the eyes. Could I die with this person? If this is the end, if these are our last living minutes on earth . . .

Is the cable about to snap? The thin thread that binds us? Is this fragile cage about to plunge, unobstructed, into the heart of the earth?

With everything so hazardous, why bother taking care at all?

You anticipate the final shudder. Either it will, or it won't work again. The short rise or the long drop. But for now there is just the intolerable wait.
You look at the man. He turns away.
The lift hums again.
The journey is over.
(This particular journey.)

Out in the sunlight you laugh. People stare.

A man in an ambulance screaming towards the grave; the attending nurse notices his face twisted with convulsions.
'Laughter? You're laughing? This is the final journey, man, you should be praying to your maker!'
'Lady, it's the same thing,' he whispers through his tears.

5 Letter from London

It was Guy Fawkes Day last weekend: 'Remember Remember the Fifth of November.' And I remembered it was almost this time last year that I met you – leftover fireworks exploding all over the city. Hard to believe it was that long ago. Hard to believe it was only that long. It's been a fuck of a year for almost everyone I know. Various friends in various states of decay: cancer, miscarriage, abortion, bankruptcy.

And me.
And the marriage.
We can't live together, can't live apart. I this *huit clos*? (Is this melodrama?) Is this modern marriage . . . ?

We sold the flat, bought another, then sold that and got a small house – Chelsea to Chiswick to Notting Hill.

Then he moved into a friend's place who was going to New York for a month. Then he returned.
Then I moved out and rented a room.

Moving. Moving. Anywhere.
Trying to find a place to be happy.
Together. Apart. Together.

I've just rented a cottage in the north of the city near the Heath. I'll keep a key to his place. And he'll take a key to my cottage. He's giving me his clarinet so he can come and serenade me like he did when we were courting. We haven't decided yet who gets the dog; she loves *him* best but I'm the one who takes care of her . . . Females are perverse sometimes.

Sometimes life simply doesn't seem real.

Moorgate, Bishopsgate, Cripplegate: all the gates into this city. How amused you were by the place names. Highgate. Billingsgate. The stories trapped in simple words . . . Words I keep returning to. Perhaps they are the only things which do not disappoint.

I was in Prague last month – the conference. I kept expecting you to appear. It was magic. Full of near crises, misunderstandings. Everyone spoke in English, though there were only four of us – an Australian, a Brit, an American and me – for whom it was our true language.

Prague is a beautiful city, but so poor. We spent one whole night dancing in a pavilion beside the river while the band played – yes, you guessed it – 'The Blue Danube'. We, the foreign visitors; there were no Czechs in sight except official representatives.

All around us, everywhere we went, were TV lights and cameras mirroring the full moon like a polka-dotted veil across the surface of the water. Lots of press, publicity. Lots of intrigue. You talk too long to one person – an Arab or Israeli, a Russian or American – and some official suddenly swoops in and spirits you off. I kept feeling I'd done something wrong. Said something wrong. But it didn't matter. Nothing mattered. That was the game.

It gave me an insight into conferences – what you were going through when we met. Con fer ence. Con: Medieval Latin meaning 'with'. Today it means 'a fraud, hoax, sham or lie'. Funny that. Isn't it? You were never much interested in words. At least that's what you said: judge by the deed, not the word. But in the end there was no deed. And so, again, words proved supreme; it was to words that you were wedded. Fidelity: *fides,* faith.

I met some wonderful people there: poets, philosophers, politicians. Some had been imprisoned for their speeches. One man I met had been exiled. Needless to say, I was the lightweight. But even that didn't matter. I was the youngest. And unaccompanied. And somehow it seemed all right, for once, to be a mascot, a muse (amuse).

I wonder how things are with you. It was nice of you to let me know – your cryptic note arrived just before I left for Prague – about your wife. I didn't think you had such a sense of humour; you always seem so . . . earnest. Though how can one say, after knowing someone for such a short time? Given her betrayal, have you also finally broken your ten-year fidelity? What's scary is how easy it is to do when you finally make the decisions. And how meaningless it all becomes. Both the fidelity and the breaking of it.

I've wondered ever since – was it a woman she had the affair with? A bit baroque perhaps. But that was my first thought. I can't see anyone passing you up for another man. And you did say, when I said I thought I hated men, that your wife had said the same thing once. And with three small boys, well, who can blame her?

Have you managed to keep it together? After your heroic act of renunciation. After that lofty speech about the marriage bond and the trust and the tie that gets stronger as it gets tighter . . . You had so much more at stake than I did. Of course, now that things are crumbling I want a child. All the nights we wasted arguing, and now it's *me* that wants the child and *he* that doesn't. Sometimes I'm afraid that I will leave it all too late, that all the possibilities will slip away while I'm still looking in the wrong place. You are lucky to have three children. All with bright blond hair, I'll bet.

How is it these days, your hair? I should have played Delilah to your Samson one of those nights we spent talking. I often thought if you'd begun to lose it – that long, languid hair, that crowning glory of which you were so proud – if it had started falling out or fading to a dirty grey, if it had started going last year, you wouldn't have resisted me.

I remember thinking that, as I left you on the steps of your hotel that afternoon, the day after the night you said you wanted to spend the whole of the next day in bed with me.

When I arrived that morning, and you ushered me into the room, ducking into the hall to finish the telephone call you were having, I remember thinking then: this won't work. Something's wrong. This is the first time I've seen him in daylight. This Aryan god with his golden hair, he could burn a pagan heart to ash. (I didn't realize then that Jews could be blond too.)

And then you insisted we go for a walk, and explained it was *her* on the phone. And then the homily on marriage. And then parting on the steps with a quick peck on the cheek. And your exit line, your older-wiser-man-of-the-world and probably well-worn exit line, your:

'What you do with this will be a measure of your maturity.'

Maturity. I think it is one of the great myths. You expect the years to wrap around you. You expect maturity to accrue, like interest on your savings, like rings around a tree.

I don't believe it anymore. I think we simply learn to imitate an image of maturity. Or perhaps we learn to mask its absence, to hide the fear and greed and impatience. It doesn't mean these aren't presiding still, they simply operate more subtly.

That morning when we met for the last time, what I wanted to say to you and your pious little homily was: Fuck You. Just Fuck You . . . But of course that's the one thing you wouldn't let me do. And so the ubiquitous Oedipal itch remains unscratched: to steal the husband from the wife, to steal the father from the mother, to have the father fuck the daughter. I'm sure it is a scene you've played before: the older man tantalizing a willing younger woman. Although in truth, I must confess, I suppose I've played the younger woman's role before as well. But I play my parts to the hilt, none of your paternal restraint, your last-minute withdrawals.

I still wonder why you didn't risk it. Just that once. It would have been so easy, safe – a married woman, different country, different continent. You aren't much of a gambler, though there was a risk of sorts in toying with the scene at all. I hate half measures – neither cowardice nor courage – there's no story in the middle ground. So . . . what is left? Eating, sleeping, working.

Work is a great opiate, isn't it? As soon as I moved out it became easier to work – except for the smothering loneliness.
Sometimes I dread being alone.
Sometimes I revel in the cleanness of it.
Sometimes I think I'll get a dog. Protection. Companionship. Another body in the bed. A reason for getting up in the morning.

Funnily enough that was another of our constant arguments: his bloody dog. I hated the dog-shit, and dog hairs and doggie smells all over the place. And I knew I would end up looking after it. In fact, when you consider all the time you spend feeding and walking and shopping for dog food, and cleaning up dog hairs, and bathing the thing, it's really not much different from a lover. And it wouldn't solve the problem of sex. Unless one were willing to entertain practices I'm not yet ready to try.

Still, I like the iconography of it – of dogs – of other things.

Dogs suggest fidelity; they also imply laziness.

Pearls indicate a virgin, they are also the jewel of the whore.

Parrots are the icon of lascivious old men, though Oliver keeps a parrot in his garden and he's neither lascivious nor old. He says that, next to apes and dolphins, parrots are the most intelligent animals on earth. He says they can distinguish colours and shapes. Are these signs of intelligence? Do these abilities make for companionship? Perhaps I should give up on men and dogs and get myself a parrot. I could call it Joe, after you: all talk and no action, the mimic of maturity.

My current lover is also a Joe. Perhaps that's why I chose him: one Joe got away, one Joe was snared – a balance for posterity; one wipes the other off the scorecard.

It still amuses me that so many of you Jews assume the name of the Virgin's husband. No, I haven't forgotten that Christ was Jewish too. Joseph, the faithful husband, trudging discreetly behind the fêted Mother and Child. Naive? Perhaps. But was it gullibility or simply pragmatism? Perhaps it wasn't such a hardship for an old man to take on a young girl, even if she was pregnant with someone else's child. One mustn't forget the brothers and sisters who followed after that virgin birth.

Think of him: quietly tending the donkey, sharpening his tools – I once sawed the legs off a chest of drawers – the sense of mystery, of power . . . Think of him selecting his wood, sawing it, planing it, nailing the crosspiece to the upright. Fathers aren't to be trusted. Our Father . . . Remember Cronos, that old god of fertility who castrated his own father and swallowed his own sons . . . And so on down to Joseph, the quiet carpenter, a specialist in noughts and crosses: noughts for him, crosses for his bastard son. So it was a gamble. Thirty-three years the kid lived – it might have died in infancy. In any case he won the toss – surely he was happier than some anonymous bachelor?

My Joseph is a gambler too. He comes from a rich family. He looks rich, dresses rich, he behaves rich, but he never has any money. At first I assumed he was keeping it all for himself, till one day he took me to the dogs and lost half a grand on a single bet. I realized then where the money went. He threw down five hundred-pound notes. He barely even watched the race. And when the winner crossed the line while his dog was still limping down the track he simply walked away.

Somebody said that all gamblers really want to lose. Somebody said that gambling was like being lost in a maze, being out of control, delivering yourself up to fate or hubris or whatever guiding force you believe in. Joe tells me that people gamble because they're ashamed of having the money. Even if it's true, that only explains the rich ones.

When I first met him I quizzed every gambler I'd ever known, trying to work out why he did it. Now I simply go with it. The whole thing seems rather masochistic; indeed my last gambler was one of those men who liked to receive pain. Better to receive than to give, as far as pain is concerned, I feel. I didn't actually indulge him myself – the odd little whack with a hairbrush or shoe – but it made me uneasy. Who was the masochist? Who was the sadist? Who was forcing whom to do what . . . ? Which is one of many reasons why that particular affair didn't last.

Of course this thing with Joe is also doomed. Still, it's interesting for now. The enduring legacy of growing up in a small town: anything to avoid boredom. Not that you'd know about such driving passions.

I had my appendix removed last month. In Marrakesh. You see, already it's not the body you knew: this one has a scar arcing from the hip towards the *Mons Veneris,* the Mountain of Venus which you never scaled. Better in Marrakesh than in Montreal or Manhattan: at least it was an experience. The banality of a routine appendectomy takes on the guise of adventure in a foreign clinic. You, I'm sure, would prefer the sterile certainty of a four-star private hospital . . . Of course it would never have worked out between us.

There are three ponds on the Heath, a short walk from where I now live. The women-only pond is the farthest away; I've never actually found it although I know it's there. The men-only I've stumbled across. I should have spotted the clues long before I actually hit the water: the flashing white of naked buttocks, scattered across the meadow like petals from a windblown rose. I will not stray that way again. The mixed pond, which is the busiest, is also the nearest to my cottage.

The water in the ponds is brown, like the rivers of my childhood; brown with leaves and pine cones and the rotting bark of logs. Every year there is a scare in the local papers: the water is poisoned, the swimming pools should be shut down. Every year a few pregnant mothers are reported giving birth to deformed babies after swimming in the pond. Some say it's the rats urinating in the water. Perhaps it is the children.

Every year I think perhaps it's time I gave up swimming in the pond. But by mid-June or July I've succumbed to the heat. Perhaps I'm a gambler too. The pond is so much nicer than any public pool. The green overhanging, the umbrella of sky, the echoing forests, the uncertain edges, the depths and sudden currents, the warm spots and cold veins, the fish nibbling your toes, brushing against your arms and legs, the ducks and drakes and fallen branches bobbing about. And still the water flows. This is the most important thing. It isn't contained. It bubbles up from somewhere and disappears again, so each minute you are swimming in a different stream.

Anyway, the ponds will be freezing over soon in this November gloom.

This was meant to be just a short note.
Just to let you know I've moved. Again.
I didn't intend it to be such a spew.

But there we are . . . There I am, at least.
Where are you?
Love – etc.
(Or whatever . . .)

6 Rivers of the Mind

You could say she asked for it. You could say: what do you expect? Women hitching. You could say: what's a man to do? This girl in jeans by the side of the road approaches, pleading, begging, she was begging for it: please, she said, please get me out of here, I've been on this roadside five and a half hours and I'm terrified of nightfall.

It's a gamble. Sure, you could say she asked for it, but what's a girl to do?

We were stuck outside Istanbul. We had been there for several hours and night was falling fast. Anna had the idea of flagging down some English trucker at the nearest petrol station. We walked and walked and finally found a place. Among the lines of lorries stacked up in the parking lot were two with GB tattooed on their flanks.

We figured the drivers must be in the restaurant. We waited round for them. Lots of other men came out: truckers looking at us, pointing, some of them saying things about us, luckily in languages we didn't speak.

Finally the Brits appeared. They were mates; did this run together every month, Birmingham to Ankara and back. I don't remember what they were transporting: food, something cold, probably sheep, goat, meat. It didn't matter. We explained that we'd been stuck there for hours, asked if they would give us a lift. A look passed between them. We noted the look but frankly, what other hope was there? They said, sure, hop in. The skinny one took us both, said he could make room for two, said he assumed we'd rather stay together. He was right.

We drove, high above the highway. We didn't talk much. He seemed happier with silence. We were tired so it all seemed fine. Dusk came, then dark. We nodded, dozed. About 2.00 am his mate flashed from behind and our man pulled over on the verge with the other truck behind him. They were stopping for a brew-up. The friend pulled a kerosene stove from under his seat. We all had tea then they said they were retreating to the cabs for a quick kip till dawn.

The cabs each had two beds behind the driver's seat, one above the other, like kids' bunks. Our driver said we could each sleep in one cab. I suggested that Anna and I would be happy to squeeze into a single bunk. But the man said, no, the bunks wouldn't take the weight. I pointed out that the two of us together probably weighed less than either of them alone; Anna was particularly thin since she only ate white food. But the man was adamant: one body per bunk. I suggested we sleep in the back, but he said it was illegal. Anyway you wouldn't want to ha ha it was refrigerated, he said. We'd freeze with all the other carcasses in there. He added we were perfectly at liberty to sleep outside if we liked, but the wild dogs in this part of Bulgaria . . .

There was nothing else for it . . . Anna went with the other guy. He hadn't taken part in the negotiations. He had watched on, silent, looking amused. He seemed OK. He packed up the stove, took a slash against the back tyre, then hauled himself up into the cab. She climbed up behind him and they disappeared behind the closed door.

My guy made a big play about fixing up my bunk, lending me his only blanket. I said I was fine, I didn't want to incur obligations, but he insisted. He took the top bunk; it creaked and groaned as he sank into it. I figured then that he must usually sleep in the bottom one, where I was.

Once we were alone, settled in the cab, in the dark, on the edge of the highway, he suddenly started to talk. Friendly, he seemed; he seemed perfectly friendly. Asked about myself and my friend. I told him we'd met the previous year – first year in college. It was true. He seemed interested: what did we do on weekends, evenings, what did we study, what did we hope to be when we grew up . . . I was afraid at first he might be jealous, but he didn't seem to be. Perhaps because we were foreign. Perhaps he even figured out we were Canadian. Perhaps he didn't care, he knew from the accent that we weren't British, he didn't seem to care about our nationality beyond that. I made it all sound as boring as possible, kept on yawning, hoping he would go to sleep. I even tried snoring, but he just kept right on talking, asking questions; it seemed rude not to answer.

Then he started on about his own life. It was what he wanted all along. He wanted to talk about his own life. Wife. No kids. They lived in a new development in the country. He was worried, he said. About her, his wife. He'd bought her a dog to keep her company while he was away on the road. A great big Alsatian to protect her. He was away two weeks out of four: long time for a woman to be on her own.

Some instinct prompted me to steer off this topic. I asked about the neighbours, the local town, the countryside, but he kept coming back to the wife, the dog. Soon as he gave her the dog she went off sex.

I'm sure it isn't related.

He was sure it was.
She's having it off with the dog. I know. Don't try to deny it. All you women stick together defending some slag you don't even know.

I don't believe a woman would do it with a dog.

What do *you* know? I saw it in a film once: Germans, Nazi officers, they knew what was what. Kept a pack of dogs, Alsatians, like the one that I got her. Threw 'em in with the women prisoners. Loved it. You could see they loved it. Much more common than you think.

I tried not to think at all.

A silence fell, then: hey, hey, you down there, why don't you come up and give me some company? Hey, I've got a problem; I've got a lazy lob. Hey, we can play dogs. I'll be the dog and you can be my wife. No I'll be me and you can be my wife.

No, I said. Go to sleep. You're making it up. You're being silly. Women aren't like that.

Women. Don't tell me about women. I know women. Do it with anything, milkman, a tramp, with doorknobs. They do. Hey, you come up here I'm coming down I'll show you.

Why don't you talk to her about it? Have you talked to her about it? Why don't you speak to your priest/doctor/mother-in-law? Perhaps she's upset that you spend so much time on the road. Perhaps she's jealous. Perhaps she thinks that you get up to things . . .

Thinks I can't do it. That's what she thinks. Spend two weeks out of four alone on the road, when a man gets home he wants his wife. I could pick up sluts on the road, you wouldn't believe the baggage, the tarts, the slits who line up on the motorway just dying for it. Come out from the cities, real classy women. Afternoon's entertainment for them. Bit of rough. That's what they like, a bit of adventure. It's the unknown. Whores, the lot of them. I'm coming down.

No, don't. Go to sleep.

I'm coming down.

I'm asleep.

No you're not. What do you think, you can stop us on the road you can hitch along with us, how many miles thousands of miles I've transported you and your friend for what for nothing nothing's for nothing what am I asking for hardly a thing a little comfort a little human companionship – natural isn't it? – what's wrong with that?

And so it went on.
I'm going to shoot that dog when I get home. That's what I'm going to do.

On and on.
I'm coming down.
There isn't room; you'll break the bunk.
You think you can just come in here, crawl into my cabin . . . That dog, I know you women . . .

Occasionally he'd drift off, snoring like a ox, then he'd wake with a quick yelp and begin.
Women, bitches, all the same. Going to kill that bitch first thing. You think I won't? Just watch me. Don't even need a gun. This Big Mother . . . I'll smash the dog, grind it into the tarmac before she knows what hit it; a smear on the tyre, a spot on the road, that's all you'll know of that dog.

I didn't sleep.

He didn't come down, although he continued threatening off and on.

As dawn broke he went quiet. Don't say nothing to your friend eh? he muttered into the spreading pink. It was just a joke. Don't you tell her, eh? Don't say nothing to my mate. The dog. It was just a joke. Didn't mean nothing by it.

A few minutes later his mate banged on the cab. My man heaved himself out of his bunk, grunting. He was wearing his trousers. He'd kept them on all the time. If only I'd known I wouldn't have been so nervous. They went round to the back of the truck for a pee.

Anna climbed up beside me: how'd you sleep? She was fine; not a peep out of her man from the moment she climbed into the bunk. A little cold, that was all. He hadn't offered a blanket. No chatter, no conversation, a quick goodnight and they both fell asleep.

I told her about the night I'd put in.

Did we ask for it? Did we deserve it? What do you expect? Two girls, two students, should have known better. It's the price you pay.

It could have been a man in a BMW playing Mahler's *Songs of the Earth*, talking Socrates, offering a candlelit dinner in a small, rural restaurant, a detour to a place he knew, a rowboat, rowing across the lake in moonlight: a sentimental journey, some summer place he'd been forty years before when he was a child, twenty years before when he was a young man courting.

Then the quiet drive home to his house – it being too late to go back on the road – where his wife would lead us to the spare bedroom: two narrow cots with crisp linen sheets. It could have been. It had been. It had happened once, it could have happened again. It still could some day.

At the first petrol stop we got out, got our stuff, said we would find another lift. My man looked destroyed: you told her, he muttered. Don't say you didn't; I know you did. You bitch you treacherous bitch. I'm going to do it, he shouted out of the open window as they headed off down the highway. Just you wait; see if I don't.

And you think: am I responsible? If this happens, if he does indeed murder the bitch, am I in some small part to blame?

The bitch? The dog? Is this man going home to murder his wife?

7 The East River

Sky-scraper: '*gratte-ciel*'. You can almost hear the buildings scraping against the sky. Birds pecking at the roofs of their cages. Notes pushing back the surrounding space. The body under the water banging against the ceiling of ice.

Right after college I moved to Manhattan. Everyone does. If only for a summer.

That time I lived on Elizabeth Street, just west of the Bowery, on the edge of Little Italy. My friends refused to visit me there, horrified by the squalor, the piles of vomit glistening in the street, sprouting like melanomas, multiplying overnight then drying up and fading away: old scabs on the skin of the street, replaced by new lesions each day.

That and the drunks in the gutters, every morning calling out for you, holding out their hats and hands, moaning and begging. How can you bear the drunks? my friends would ask, appalled. The alkies, the winos, the rubby-dubs gather like garbage in the streets, leaning against each other, propped up by hydrants or telephone poles, leaking urine, feeding fleas.

Frankly, I quite liked the drunks. The smell was a small price to pay for the security they provided: a bodyguard squad, always there, watching, waiting for something to happen, dying for a scene, an event, a diversion, something to fill those vacant eyes. Always in the alleys, in the ditches, on the curbs. Everywhere you looked they were there: behind every garbage can, under every pile of litter, inside every cardboard box casually tossed into the street. They would simply climb inside, inhabit them where they lay. Rapists, muggers, even burglars preferred the privacy of the Upper East Side to the public forum of the Bowery.

That summer I did odd jobs: worked in an editor's studio in the Bliss Building midtown for a few weeks, but then I mislaid for the umpteenth time a crucial two frames of the show we were cutting. It was an hour-long documentary about a dissident Macedonian preacher who spoke no English and was trying to set up a colony in Massachusetts.

What endures is the sound of his endless muttering. On and on. Backwards and forwards, it sounded the same. Lips moving, glued to the words, defying any distortion: forwards or backwards, fast forward or real time. The only memorable thing about him was his blue polka-dot tie; he wore it anywhere, everywhere and completely without fail. We figured it must have been a farewell present from some mother or lover before he defected.

But after I lost yet another two frames – let me point out that a frame is no more than the size of a fingernail so it isn't that difficult to mislay – after I misplaced two frames of the man mid-blink or mid-sneeze or mid-opening his mouth for another incomprehensible pronouncement, the editor figured my heart wasn't in it and suggested I look for work somewhere else. 'Perhaps it's his Christianity which is bugging you,' he suggested. 'Perhaps unconsciously you want to thwart the project because he's a preacher.' The editor had been in analysis for twenty years.

Perhaps it's his polka-dot tie, I muttered, slipping a few extra frames of the film into my bag as I left.

Like all good Americans faced with an uncertain future, I headed west that afternoon; I wandered along some axis till it ran out at the edge of the island and there was the Circle Line Boat Tour in front of me. So I signed on for a tour of the city I'd been living in for the past few months.

The East River, the Hudson River, the Harlem River. It wasn't till I'd circled Manhattan that I realized it is an island simply by virtue of three narrow rivers. For all its splendid isolation, it's simply sliced away from the continent by three little strips of water.

When it started to rain I stayed up on deck. The rain was hot, sticky. One other person remained up there with me: a short, grey man in a large raincoat. He was Latvian, a Latvian Jew.

By the time the boat hummed past the landfill of New Jersey he had told me all the ways he managed to survive. In Zurich he had offered his body as a nude 'life' model for art classes. Then he worked as an undertaker's assistant because the money was good and the work allowed him to study anatomy. There was also the added perk, I discovered, of free rings and cufflinks from the crematees: 'Well, darling, it was just going into the fire otherwise. You can hardly call it stealing; I was preserving the pieces for posterity.'

Then his girlfriend objected to the everpresent odour of formaldehyde so he moved on to dealing: 'Pictures, darling; art not narcotics.' But for reasons which I never fathomed he suddenly left Europe for Manhattan.

There he worked on the docks, unloading ships till he broke his arm. Then he sold his blood to get enough cash to purchase some stock: 'Pictures, books, antiques: it's all commodities, you might as well be selling haemorrhoid cream.'

After several months – either he had a lot of blood to sell or he talked them into an extremely good price: 'I'm a Jew, darling, it's in the blood; it has to be or else we die' – he began selling paintings from the back of a borrowed car in TriBeCa.

To get his green card though he had to have a real employer. Since the only skill he could market was his HGV licence, for three years he worked the graveyard shift transporting chickens from upstate New York to the slaughterhouses north of Chelsea.

'And at present' – I sensed we were getting to something important now because he paused – 'at present, I am a private dick.' He said the phrase straight, as though it were made up of real words, not some comic-book jargon.

Heavens, I said. I couldn't think of anything else to say.

'I could get you an assignment if you like,' he added. At that moment the tour ended and the other passengers began scurrying up from the hold, onto the teetering ladder, to disappear over the edge of the boat.

Sure, I said, and gave him my number.

Then he suggested we go for a coffee. The rain had stopped and it wasn't yet dark so I let him lead me to a Portuguese place in the meat district. The room was airless as a tomb. We sat at a table by the open door as the trucks lumbered past pushing waves of hot, dead breath into our faces.

'As a matter of fact . . .' he said as he poured half a cup of sugar into his coffee, then took a napkin from the dispenser, folded it neatly in half and used it to soak up the extra liquid that had slopped into the saucer. This gesture, the slightly self-conscious neatness, the precision of it, was curiously touching. I figured that no murderer would take such trouble to wipe up his coffee spills.

'As a matter of fact . . .' he said, 'I have a little job right now which might be of interest.'

Oh?

'Let me make you an offer you can't refuse,' he said.

'Have you ever watched the sun set from the top of the Cor Covado?' he said.

'A samba that doesn't bring sadness is like a wine that doesn't bring drunkenness . . .' It was a loose translation of a line from a samba by Jobim: *'Et pourtant une samba sans tristesse c'est comme un vin qui ne donne pas l'ivresse . . .'* I recognized the quote.

He explained that he was tailing an adulterous couple, a couple whom he presumed to be adulterous. Company policy wouldn't let the investigators know the charge, so they couldn't manufacture or distort the evidence. But he'd already sussed the case.

He was tailing a man who was with a woman who didn't look like a wife. His orders were to chart their movements, see if they entered the same room every night, emerged from the same room every morning. No photos required, no tape recordings. The job was a doddle, simply a statement: yes or no, did they sleep together? He figured it was the woman's husband or perhaps the man's wife who had hired him.

The couple were booked into a fancy hotel in Rio for three days and the dick needed an escort to make him less conspicuous. 'A single man in a holiday hotel would stick out like a sore thumb.' He blushed as he said it, rushing to ensure that I didn't assume that he was assuming . . . 'A strict business deal. In public we appear as man and wife; in private you can do what you like. Shared room, separate beds. One hundred bucks a day and all expenses paid.'

We arranged to meet at the Varig desk at JFK that evening.

At 6.45 pm I turned up at the check-in wearing a linen dress, matching shoes and a suitcase with enough clothes in it to pass as a Manhattan housewife.

He wasn't there.

Was there a mistake?
Was he suddenly pulled off the case?
Was he waiting in some other line, in some other terminal, cursing me?
Was he lying ill somewhere, dying in some gutter, a knife in his back, a gun at his temple, unable to telephone and explain?

Rio de Janeiro: River of January. Janus: the two-faced deity, staring backwards into the future, peering forwards into the past. Or was he just another double-dealing joker?

Cor Covado, Ipanema, all the glossy photographs: nut-brown chests and asses spread across the gleaming sand like peaches, bound by the thin cords of fluorescent bathing costumes.

No, I haven't seen the sun set from the top of Cor Covado. Yet.

8 Mind the Gap

Memory: that gap between the train and the station platform; that infinitesimal little lip that can suddenly suck you in.

On the wall opposite his sofa was a picture of a goat, a charcoal sketch he bought from one of his patients; a survivor of Auschwitz. The first evening I saw the thing it looked like a devil, an evil demon staring me down. But by morning it appeared quite harmless.

Over the next few days I watched the goat's expression change from irritation to amusement, from disapproval to surprise. Sometimes it was a benign nanny watching indulgently over us; sometimes it was a malevolent billy seeking sordid mischief.

He was a Manhattan analyst; he liked to chart my differing responses to the goat.

One night the goat climbed off the wall and joined us on the sofa. Its hair was soft as cashmere. It had a sort of halo which I'd always assumed was smudges in the drawing, but down here, on the cushions beside me, I realized it was a sort of eerie light which hovered round the goat's head.

That night the goat was indisputably a billy, shoving his pointed little organ up and down along every surface. My friend got quite upset at the poor creature, throwing him onto the floor at one point when he inadvertently stepped on his thigh. Goat's hooves pack a punch – sharp little things which pinch the flesh. But the goat jumped right back into the fray, undaunted by my friend's annoyance.

I didn't mind the faint odour of stable, though my friend was afraid it would linger for days, and of course it was his place, not mine. But after a few hours of cavorting – they say a goat will eat anything; I can vouch for that . . . And those quick little tongues are as strong as fish. But eventually, when everyone was sated, we all dropped where we lay, the goat with its head in my lap and it's haunches spread across my friend's buttocks while he slept, face-down, on the floor.

At dawn I noticed that the goat seemed to be a nanny again. In the first light I saw her lying on her side with my friend sucking at her breast. Is it a fantasy? A memory? Perhaps that was simply a dream.

By morning the goat had returned to its frame on the wall. Nimble creature. The only testament to our capricious menage was a row of tiny footprints on the wall leading up to the picture frame, and a lingering odour – not quite of the stable, but certainly more animal than vegetable.

Guernica. The Holocaust. The goat, the bull, the horses. The unexpected victim: the horse, paralyzed between the swirl of a naked woman riding astride it and the demented bull preparing to charge it. And behind them the toreadors flapping like handkerchiefs in the wind: waving? drowning? calling for help?

The disembowelled horse, vulva-wound sucking the bull's phallic horn, bleeding drops like diamonds shattering onto the dirt of the ring while the bull looks on, bewildered, in its brutish helplessness.

Me? Was that me? Picasso may have asked of the trail of braying horses. Yes perhaps; perhaps that painting is mine, there were so many. Could it have belonged to Matisse?

They came, you know, they came to the bullfight, nobody forced them to come. They quivered to the scent of blood. It was always the women who kicked and scratched to secure a ringside seat. And the ears, they screamed for the ears, soft like a spaniel's cheek, dripping thick as claret, spotting their velvet trousers and hunter-green capes. Are you sure it's mine? It looks like Matisse. I had several of Henri's works. I can't remember now. Yes, if you say, it probably is mine. Does it matter? Of course he copied me, or maybe I copied him; it's hard to tell any more.

Was it Marie-Thérèse or Dora Maar; the woman who cried? I loved her red nails. What colour is her hair? That will tell us. Is it dark or fair? You can't see? Surely you can say what colour her hair is? Oh, I'm too tired. My eyes are going. I can't remember what colour her hair was, none of them. Was it Sylvie with the hair pulled back like a Greek vase painting, like a goat's tail? Was it Sylvie with the goat's tail? She was so young. I painted her naked. Never touched the girl. Did I? What difference does it make anyway, they're all dead now. Like me.

I once knew a man who walked down the street and ran into a woman he'd known in Barcelona years before. He couldn't remember her name. She had been a secretary in one of the international organizations. He couldn't remember her name, he couldn't remember the name of her boss or her job or how well he'd known her. She blushed when they stopped to talk to each other, but what really bothered him about it was that he couldn't remember whether they had fucked or not all those years before.

He had a momentary flash, a memory of muslin blowing in from an iron balcony. The back of a woman's legs stretched out across the bare sheets in the heat of the afternoon siesta. Downy hair on her buttocks. Streaks of blood, brown like rust, like the strokes of a watercolour brush on the insides of her thighs. Blood on the towel she'd insisted they place on the bed before making love.

Her face on its side, buried under her arm, cast aside, stretched to the corners of the bed like St Catherine on her wheel, on her rack. Her hair: was it black? Was it blond? Matted and tangled, it had tumbled in a sweaty river down her back.

He had a flash but he couldn't remember her hair. Was it black? Was it blond? And what would that tell anyway? This woman walking down Bond Street with her umbrella on a rainy March morning. So what if he could remember an afternoon in Barcelona twenty years before? If he could see the colour of her hair through her garish silk scarf, spotted brown with drops of rain? So what would that tell him anyway? So she blushed. And they talked of the weather.

Then he smiled rather sadly and hurried off.

The places you remember aren't necessarily the ones which seem nicest at the time. I keep returning to Punt Alla. Off-season. An Italian holiday resort, all boarded up and shuttered like a Marguerite Duras film. The sadness of resort towns out of season, devoid of significance. You can almost hear the ghosts of children shouting on the sandy paths between the shivering cottages. This must have been in November; the leaves were off the trees and even Florence looked bereft.

I'd had an argument that morning with my travelling companion. Was it Joe? No, we never travelled together. Was it my husband? Or Oliver? No, it was a lover. Perhaps it was the Danish poet: my first boyfriend, more or less. Every trip we took it rained. Not that it matters now who the man was. What I recall of that trip was the place.

The friends we were visiting wanted to check on their summer house. My companion and I had no desire to be alone, so we crowded into the back of the car with their two children. We remained silent, the man and I, at either end of the narrow car seat with someone else's children bickering between us.

The town was empty, dry, dead. It looked cheap and faded. The cottages were smaller than I'd imagined, thin-walled, clapboard, paint already peeling, revealing duller reds beneath the faded greens and browns which seemed to be the favoured colours of the summer past.

I went off to walk on my own on the beach. But before long the rest of them followed: first the children, still squabbling; then the parents earnestly discussing; finally the man I was with – wasn't with – was fighting with – aimlessly tagging along at the rear.

Suddenly, as we rounded a point, there was a café – a wooden hut with rickety tables and chairs on the beach in front. As we approached it an old man emerged. By the time we reached the hut he had poured out carafes of wine and piled straw baskets full of bread. It was a fisherman's café, but since there were no fishermen that day, with the wind and the rain, he set out to hook us: a fisher of men.

No menu was offered, there was no discussion of what or how much. He simply appeared a few minutes later with a platter of grilled fish. In the wind, in the slowly showing sun, in the salt-smelling air. We passed plates and filled glasses. The old man joined us. My lover and I sat side by side; our Italian friends interpreted. It became one of those rare occasions.

Remember this. You must remember this. When everything else is gone and we have become strangers, remember this moment. I know I've said the lines before. I don't recall to whom or in what circumstance.

I have friends who have been in analysis for up to fifteen years: almost as many years striving to remember as struggling to forget. When I point out that, despite all the money and the angst and the days and weeks and months and years of lying, crying on the analyst's couch, they are still unhappy and unfulfilled –

'Ah,' they reply, 'but you didn't know me before.'

I used to swim naked in the moonlight in a pond in Vermont with a boy, now a man with two children and a wife of his own.

One summer we borrowed a farmhouse and spent a month being hippies. We picked berries in the meadow and I made wild strawberry jam while he hauled logs and cut wood and laid fires. We used to make love in a shaft of sun which came through the high cathedral-like windows and spread across the wooden floor of our sitting room every afternoon.

Then we'd have a picnic in the barley field, or hike into the village, or read on the bench outside the back door until nightfall.

Then we'd walk hand in hand down to the pond, slip off our clothes and slide into the water.

Once the moon was shining full, a round yellow disc, like saffron, like honey, shimmering on the pond's clear surface. All night as the stars melted we took turns diving from a rock. Each dive would shatter the mirror-calm, fracturing the moon into a shower of gold coins, raining down over the water like phosphorescent net.

The man is now an analyst living in Manhattan.
Did I say that already?
He has two children and a wife. And a picture of a goat on the wall in his consulting room.

The goat is a symbol of the damned. At the Last Judgement Christ will appear and separate the sheep from the goats, the believers from the sceptics. In that particular equation, I'm afraid I must cast my lot in with the goats.

Betrayal? Who is betraying whom? He is the doctor, I am the patient. (I prefer to think of myself as a 'client'; it sounds more powerful. He calls me his patient though, because, he says, I am in pain.) Who has the authority in this particular relationship?

Besides, it's only for old times, he says each time we do it.
You understand, this doesn't mean a thing.
I understand.

9 A Lie Is Sometimes an Apology in Disguise

Lying there, legs spread, him inside me halfway to his elbow. I wondered what his wife would say if she could see us now.

Please sir, is it . . . is it all right?

I see the thinning patches at the back of his head. The secret part he thinks nobody knows about, the thing he wakes from nightmares fearing: loss. It's going. He's losing it, hair by precious hair. But he thinks that nobody else can see it.

Please sir . . .

He tells me to get up. Like adults we sit face to face. No, not like adults: he sits behind the desk and talks.

She listens. Like a student with her professor. Like the artist and his model. He watches her. It's very common this. He charts her responses. It's very common this.

This . . .?

A slight abnormality, that's all. Nothing serious.

She knows that if she can just make him love her, if she can just seduce him, if she can just entice him to succumb, he won't let her die . . .

Of course we all fell in love with our professors. Our analysts, teachers, doctors, priests. Our movie stars, our sports idols. Loved them, hated them, sought out the most intimate details: I saw him dining in the house alone with the *au pair*, I saw it, through the window as I walked past with my bicycle. Disgusting, outrageous, abusing his position John Proctor I wish he'd abused it with me.

My tutor was notorious. I suppose I sought him out for that if for nothing else and yes, I succumbed, I fell for it, I submitted to his fabled charm.

I basked in the contempt of former students now living adult lives in London – Him you have Him what a wanker, phoney. What a fraud. Yes yes tell me more, I begged; the more I betrayed him, the more I adored him. I rifled through the library, checking the card indexes, seeking out the reviews, previews, interviews, revelling in any less than glowing comments on his work. Drinking sherry or lemonade in his wood-panelled study, discussing my Hopkins or Yeats, knowing that *The Times* had said, the *Catholic Herald*, the *Baltimore Sun* had said that he was second-rate.

Loved him or hated him; it came to the same thing in the end. Another term, another crop of chattering students writing papers on poets they hadn't even read. I don't suppose he spoke my name once in that whole term.

Oh, you know, it was the usual adolescence: gawkiness, isolation. I spoke with the wrong accent, wrong vocabulary, did the wrong things on weekends and holidays, couldn't name the football team, not even the cheerleaders and even worse, my mother wore blue jeans and no lipstick. Sure, it was the sixties, but this was small town Ontario. And my limp must have set me apart, although I wasn't aware of it at the time. Nothing special really: a classic adolescence. And you?

'My loneliness was my red hair,' he murmured.
I was hooked. My first lover. He was Danish I believe.

Ballet was my passion when I was a girl. I always thought I'd be a dancer till these tits appeared. Great heaving dugs, and still they yield no milk that I've discovered. Nureyev was the ideal. I met him once. I was with a Russian friend, an old man. Another old man. A White Russian who claimed to know Rudi through some friends of friends.

Once when Nureyev was performing at Covent Garden my Russian took me backstage to see him. He said Rudi had invited us. He'd had a lunch in the country the previous week with Rudi and some balletomanes and Rudi had told him to come back for a drink when he saw the show. I suspect, when the evening came, Rudi had forgotten he'd ever even met my friend.

We had to wait at the stage door for his dresser to collect us. We seemed to walk for miles through dingy corridors up tiny stairs past insect-women scurrying from door to door.

When we finally got there the dressing room was cramped and dull. Nureyev barely even turned around. He sat in front of his mirror looking at us in the reflection, looking more at himself than at us. He offered us champagne from one of several open bottles but didn't join us in a glass. He was busy wiping off his make-up. His table was littered with round cotton pads, white at the edges, the insides pink with skin-coloured cream. Used cotton pads billowed around him like petals off a poppy.

I've never been too keen on dancers; in the flesh they always look like hairdressers or gigolos. I never really wanted to be a dancer anyway.

Looking into the rabbi's eyes you suddenly know. Potential. I could corrupt him, you think; I could corrupt this little Yiddisher, his brown eyes big as lakes you long to dive into: the pine-bottomed lakes you only find at the very top of the highest mountains, reflecting the sky; there are no clouds that high.

Naive. His naivety. He had never met anything like you, he doesn't believe you could exist, not the real thing, not a thing like you are, his naivety big as the brown eyes, trusting like a dog, faithful as a prayer shawl, upright as a pulpit.

His fat wife buttons straining from her breasts enormous chest her babies fat and hair like her bustling round the kitchen bristling. This goy this dangerous woman stealing into her husband's head behind the mask of questions, she's not dumb she doesn't speak she doesn't study but she understands. The questions are not questions they're a decoy she can smell the idea forming, the actions in rehearsal behind this talk of scholarship. She bangs and spills the kettle, offers tea up black and scalding and still he doesn't see. He scowls to her the baby's crying one several several dozen babies crying for the mother and she knows the real danger is here and the baby doesn't see it and there's nothing she can do.

Reluctantly she goes to tend the tears to change the nappies while the real danger rattles as she always knew it would right in her kitchen gleaming kitchen which she always kept so clean against the danger in her very own her territory hers her cleanliness is next to him he is an innocent on this terrain the woman's sphere he is a rookie cannon-fodder lamb to the innocently following a scapegoat goat a goat he is a fool capricious innocent and he'll never even realize.

And now she has to live with this the knowledge the contempt that he could be so and in her their her very own her kitchen her spic and span and godliness that he could be so naively contaminated by that impure untouchable that Woman.

He wouldn't know what had happened to him, you think, slowly easing apart the lids of his eyes in preparation for slipping inside, this rabbi, this preacher, this scholar of evil and good, the *Sitra Achra,* the other side, the unclean woman. I could get this man this man his family and all the pious brown-eyed men behind him and to come.

This shiksa this unclean woman this goy this temptress she could make your fears come true, she could prove the prophets the mysogynists she could make their warnings spring to life and destroy you like a virus an invisible virus which creeps into the system and suddenly weeks or months or generations later comes to life corrupting the data, destroying the machine.

I could get this man who looks at me like that so trusting so naive this pastoral counsellor from the top of his teetering stack of books I could bring them tumbling like the walls of Jericho the tower of Babel and you would never even know.

This urge . . . this urge to Destroy. This other. He could be a rabbi, a Jesuit in his stringy beard his black shirts like a nun sitting in your kitchen drinking your strong black tea. He could be . . .

More women burned as witches in two hundred years than Jews in the ovens.

He could be . . .

You could, you know it, climb into his soul and set his brain on fire. You could burn his soul to ash.

10 Break-ins

Neat little puddles, little shivers. Discreet indiscretions, like a shaving of ice or a handful of crystals, gently, deliberately, poured into a gutter at the edge of the street.

A necklace. A bracelet. A studded belt meandering along the road reminding you that you too are vulnerable, adding a frisson of excitement to the walk, in the dark, through the empty street, back to the place where you left it.

A gentle tinkling of glass, like the little cry 'shit' or 'fuck' or 'damn' uttered, muttered more than cried, when you arrive and find, yes, yet again, it was yours.

The window. The glass, shattered into a little pool. Another stud in the belt, another diamond in the bracelet to reflect someone else's fears. Somebody, somewhere is sighing with relief as you stand staring at these gleaming shards in the streetlight which is never light enough to show the culprit.

It's a gamble you take, and each time it happens, somewhere you knew it would. Somewhere you knew that this would be the time, the place. In this way, at least, you are responsible. And in the fact that you own the window that they're stealing from. In this you are always, always have been, always will be responsible. You will always have something that somebody wants.

Sometimes they just want to break it. Sometimes they just want to smash it for fun. Sometimes there's nothing left to take, or in contempt they leave what there is, just break in to show you they know you are there and you can't ever escape from them.

It's a tough way to make a living, you console yourself, wondering, even as you do, if the illicit tingle, the brush of excitement shivering up the spine each time they hear the glass hit the pavement, isn't easier than pushing pens in an air-conditioned office. Probably more lucrative too.

And when you start to wonder if the culprit isn't down the street in some doorway, behind some tree, in some other dark window, looking out, watching you. And also if he – statistically, breaking-in is one of those gender-related sports/professions/hobbies; I use the pronoun 'he' advisedly; I am not an unconscious mysanthropist . . . You start to wonder also if He is the one who did it last time. And the time before. And the time before that.

I once knew a woman who suddenly sold her terraced Georgian house and moved into a flat very high up in a tenement block in the middle of a barren plot of land on the edge of the city.

Suddenly, for no reason she would disclose, she became convinced that people were watching her, peeping in at her from her garden, spying at her from across the road. Even thirteen storeys up she was sure she could hear people tapping at her windows at night.

'It's branches from the trees,' the police suggested, but the trees didn't grow that high.

'It's grit from the polluted air,' her neighbour assured her, but even on clear days, on sunny days, on days when it had just rained and the air was clean, she could hear the taptaptapping tapping to get in.

'It's just your imagination,' her doctor said. Didn't say – implied.

One day a note came from the maintenance man asking when it would be convenient for the window washer to do her flat. She refused him permission. She refused permission for her windows to be washed. Ever.

Over the years her windows became dirtier and dirtier, until eventually the sun couldn't penetrate anymore. Cut off from all natural light, her eyesight deteriorated. The gloom expanded, her vision diminished. Eventually she went blind in the dark cavern of her flat on the thirteenth floor of a high-rise on the city's edge. It was the first time in her life that she felt safe. She couldn't see them; they couldn't see her. At least that's what she believed.

The only thing she missed was the sight of the river, slippery and black, slipping through the city like a glistening eel, with the polka-dot of barges speckling its skin. What she missed was its hot, potent breath teasing a shiver from her bare legs on hot summer evenings before she nailed the windows shut and allowed the dirt to block out the light. The sight, the feel, the smell, the touch of the river, that's what she missed; all that remained to her was the memory. But maybe that was better anyway than the real thing.

There is an old Greek proverb: one must praise one's home or else the neighbours will burn it down.

The loneliness: this power. Darling, darling, he moans as you slam into him, riding him in the semi-light from the street-lamp outside. Darling, he utters, eyes squeezed against the pleasure the pain his face like a baby's. Darling, he sighs.

But the Darling is somebody else. You hardly know each other; certainly not intimately enough to have evolved such endearments.

And suddenly in that Darling it is you who are humiliated.

Let us go back. Let us pretend we never did it. Let us be coy and shy with each other, flirting, as though we don't know what it will be like. As though it is all still before us. As though we don't know each other at all, not like this, not intimately. Then there might still be a chance for us.

The Casanovas and Don/Donna Juans are the real victims of romance; their souls invaded, their dreams consumed with the conviction that this time . . . That this will be the one true perfect . . .

The thief becomes the robbed. The victim is left with her silver ball, her silk handkerchief, her shower of gold and the memory of this fantastical creature, enthralled, this diminished creature, flaccid and shrivelled, slinking off to roll the rock of fantasy once more up to the top of that endless pedestal of faith, convinced that next time . . .

Depression. It seeps over you like an incoming tide. I moved in with a man once, a banker, a government clerk, a teacher in some second-rate university. No, 'moved in' suggests action; I didn't move in so much as I simply never left.

Night bled into day bled into night. I cooked for him, and ate, and even cleaned up, to the extent of finding the least greasy cup, plate, fork for the next meal.

In the beginning he liked the company: an audience to his accomplishments. He would leave for work in the morning and return the requisite eight hours later. I understand why he didn't kick me out: it was the joy of seeing a light in the window from the bottom of the street – it was autumn when I arrived, the clocks had just gone back: spring forward, fall back.

That pleasure as you turn the key, knowing that for once you will not be engulfed in darkness. I didn't speak much, didn't make noise, didn't bang pots and pans or splash in the bath or turn on the radio or TV, but a person, a presence, a live human being, however discreet, beats the silence. Or even a dog. I've resorted to dogs in my time; they're easier to feed than lovers, easier to keep clean.

At first that was enough for him, my presence defeating the emptiness. By the time it wasn't, I was already ensconced.

'Why don't you do something? Get a job! Do something with your time! What do you do all day?' he cried.

I didn't ask him what *he* did, so I didn't feel obliged to reply.

Occasionally I'd take the laundry to the laundromat. Better to climb into the tub and be spun silly with the smothering suds than spend two hours in that bleak fluorescence watching the clothes go round. Mostly I just slept. A woman who is tired of London . . .

Sometimes I looked out the window. O'Henry got all his stories simply by looking out his window. If I looked up I could watch the clouds – they move much faster than one expects. If I looked down I could watch the mothers pushing prams in the street. If I looked across I could watch the dogs in the park squatting to shit, their haunches quivering, the look of intense concentration as steaming sausages of faeces quietly dropped from their pulsating anuses: that extraordinary sense of accomplishment.

I want a child. I could never watch the dogs without wanting a child of my own. If I had a child I'd whip it. Whippet. Get it? It's a joke. There was a pair of whippets who used to come to the park every afternoon: such lovely, trusting, feline heads. Trusting, like children.

Most of the time I just sat and waited. All I wanted from the man was to be taken by him. From the back, from the front, from the top, from the bottom, constantly and ceaselessly. He didn't.

One morning I got bored and left. That's the real thing about depression. Suddenly, slowly, it simply retreats. The trick is to catch it on the turn, to realize it's going. It was spring. The clocks had just sprung forward, so I didn't leave him with too much darkness.

Skinny fowl with flaccid flesh beneath their black flapping dresses. Red-faced lechers, drinking indulgences.

I never knew a priest who didn't do it.

Bathed in their incense, swathed in their linen, with the fine lace mantle of dandruff drifting down from their wispy tufts of thinning hair. Yes, God has a sense of humour – so few hairs to create such a shower. Ruddy from the grunt and groan of denial, abstinence, fantasy. The lines tracing maps in their cheeks, on the bulbs of their noses. The hieroglyphs, letters, the stories: betrayal, betrayal. The ones who fumble little boys in the vestry. The little boys grow old. Did I? Did he? No, it isn't possible, an hysterical fantasy. Hysteria is a woman's indulgence: wandering womb. No it didn't happen, it couldn't have happened to me, I'm a man.

The bleak Nova Scotia evenings: Nova Scotia/New Scotland; New Amsterdam, New Caledonia, New York – didn't they realize then that nothing is ever new? Preparing for the long walk home, the slow trudge: snap snap snap. Each step echoes through the layers of ice into the plunge of snow beneath. And you want to remain on the surface, and you suck in your weight till you could float like a balloon and still the ice breaks leaving a trail of telling little boot prints, birds' feet, arrows across the field, pointing the way, identifying the prey for all the wild dogs to see.

Little boys, little girls, the wild dogs aren't choosy. The foxes and bears. The rabbis and priests and dirtyoldmen who break into your life like bandits, who smash'ngrab your soul, who slip through the holes in your aura like a bleak depression, like snow in an abandoned cabin on wintery Arctic plains.

11 Girl's Best Friend

If he doesn't go down on you the first date I say fuck him I mean life's too short to mess around. I've decided to stop wasting time: you might as well go for the essentials, right?

The smaller the man the bigger the dildo.

Jim's got a long pink wrinkled one, must be the cheapest line in the shop. When I first saw it I burst out laughing. It begs comparison. And believe me he didn't hold a candle to the cellophane-wrapped, battery-supplied, twelve-inch, pink, plastic version. In secret we girls refer to it as 'Pink Floyd' – yes, that's right, the group that died ten years ago.

John had a long bone-whitish one, made of some sort of hard rubber. It looked like a gigantic thumb, but blended perfectly with his pasty complexion. I think he thought he could slip it in without anybody noticing.

Jack had a little gold one. Like a wide-boy with a false tooth, he'd pull it out at the slightest provocation, display it to the world. It was sweet, you had to admit; it looked like a kiddie's toy; neither sinister nor ridiculous, just a little insubstantial.

Joe had a gorgeous chrome one which looked just like a Brancusi. I longed for one like that to keep my bracelets on, but he wouldn't part with it. I don't think he believed that I would really use it just for jewellery. I would have done. I keep my word. I may be an easy lay but I do not break my promises.

Simon had two; one for each hole. Thought he was an innovator. Never tried them on himself though.

All the men I know have vibrators; they keep them for their girlfriends. All the women I know use vibrators, though none of them owns one herself. Never have the guts to go in and buy one from a shop. Afraid to order from a magazine in case unsolicited porn starts pouring through the mail slot. Always use their boyfriends'. And the boyfriends never give them up: 'No, you can't take it home; use it here.'

'Perhaps I should have given you the vibrator,' R said once when I told him it was over. 'Perhaps none of this would have happened if I'd just let you take it home,' he moaned when I told him I had found someone else, someone who lived just down the road. That's the problem with north/south relationships: you spend all your time on the road inbetween. The new man could be on my doorstep in seven minutes.

So give it to me now, I suggested.

'No way.'

You don't use it yourself; what good will it be to you now that I've gone?

'I'll have to recycle it,' he sulked, clasping it to his breast.

You think you can fob off a used vibrator on your next girlfriend?!

'Why not?' he grinned, 'I did with you.'

When I was going away I used to sabotage Joe's vibrator, turning the batteries upside down so the thing wouldn't work if he tried it on some bimbo airhead piece of skirt . . . (No: much too obvious, this language of contempt, the feeble stab of the oppressed and insecure . . .) If he tried it on some one-night-stand he picked up at the tracks. He never said anything about it: 'The machine isn't working,' or, 'The batteries are dead.' That's how I knew he was faithful to me. To me and Lady Luck. Cuckold. She cheated him. Over and over, she two-timed and double-dealt him. And still he danced to her tune, jumping to serve her, poised, anticipating her beck and call.

I couldn't bear the competition so eventually I broke with him. Him and his vibrator and his cheating lady love.

One night in Paris, walking along the rue Pigalle, one night in Manhattan walking along 42nd Street, one night in London walking along Brewer Street, one night in Montreal walking along St Lawrence Main, one night in Rio walking along the Copacabana, I got the man I was with to duck into a porn shop and buy me a vibrator.

My own, my very own vibrator.

He came out a few minutes later empty-handed.
I knew it was too easy. What's the problem? I sighed; don't they stock them?
'Gold or silver?' he replied; 'I wasn't sure what colour you'd prefer.' (We'd only met the night before.)
'I imagine you're the silver type,' he suggested, 'but I didn't want to presume.'
He was right.

We used it all that week, but on our return he kept the thing. He wanted to get it engraved for me: 'For X, with love from Y./ Paris, London, New York, Rio, Montreal/ nineteen ninety-something'.

Over the next few weeks he would carry it back and forth from his place to mine in a plastic bag, each time taking it home because he hadn't yet managed to get it engraved. We broke up a few weeks later. He still hadn't managed to get it engraved. Of course. It was still in his possession. Of course. Now I have to do without. So much for my very own machine. Vibrators don't come that easily to women.

12 Casting to the Rise

Mickey Finn, Muddler, Parmachene Belle.
Silver Doctor (Mengele), Dark Montrealer.
Joe's Hopper, Hare's Ear, Hairwing Highlander.
Royal Coachman, Welshman's Button, Lady Caroline.
Cow Dung, Bitch Creek Nymph.
Black Gnat, Grey Wulff, White Millar, Red Ibis,
Whirling Blue Dun.
May Fly, Stone Fly, Caddis Fly, etc . . .

The rise: the slap of fin against water, the initial appearance, leaping from the dark, greasy depths.
The tease, the titillating nibble.
The flirting lure, the flashing bait.

The tug, the hook driving deep into flesh. The fight to pull him in, the struggle, you against him: dragging him forward, easing him on, keep your rod down, close to the water, don't pull him out yet, he might wriggle off.

Keep him calm, unsuspecting. Give him his head a little, lull him till he's close enough to catch.

Net him. Land him. Haul him in beside you. Throw him in with the others at the bottom of the boat. Watch him a moment, the colours fade so quickly: the smooth fat sheen, the sparkle and flash, diminishing each second as he flops and slaps, flaccidly, madly in the bottom of the boat. All dignity lost, all speed or grace or subtlety dying the minute he bit into your hook.

The quick snap, finger thrust down his throat; the quick snap of the neck. The priest, hanging heavy over his head, one benediction, one quick blessing and it's over.

Avoiding the gluey eyes, the gaping lips, the bloody gills gasping.

And she calls herself a vegetarian . . .

Wet flies, dry flies: no flies on this fisherwoman. No coarse fisher her. No slugs or worms or maggots prized out from the earth, she purchases her bait from the best outfitters: bright-coloured feathers, red and silver hair, bits of shiny tinsel – that's how she nabs 'em.

Dusk to dark, rowing on the inky black, the oily black lake. Whipping the water with your line, beating it; the spine of your rod poised above the rippling skin.

The false cast, the back cast. Threading out the line, dancing the fly, drawing it back in again. Over and over. As the forest draws nearer, closing in around you.

The shadows spread from the trees to the lake, slowly engulfing. Oblivious, you cast, entranced by the game. In this sport the opponents don't meet till the winner has won – a little like an arranged marriage, you could say if you wanted. Intoxicated by the potential, hovering, just beneath the surface, invisible but present. It simply requires faith. Faith, a lot of patience, a little talent, a good rod.

It's a gamble, yes, but the odds are stacked against the fish.

The silence descending.
The whisper of a rise.
The loon's cry: that distant echo of loneliness.
The nightmare crackle of a moose stumbling through the brush.
The angry slap of a beaver tail.

The night the mayfly hatches and the lake goes wild. A piscean orgy like the end of Ramadan or the carnival, *le carnival du lac* where the fishes gorge themselves on any passing dainty. The killing promiscuity. The hook in the gut, in the gills, in the eye. The flaming orange, the fluorescent blue; the flashing vulgarity which lures to the death.

Don't cast to the rise, that's an amateur's fallacy. You think the fish is going to jump twice in the very same spot? Don't you realize fish swim? They have to keep moving, just like the rest of us. You take aim and let the line sing out, with luck you hit dead centre, a bull's eye, the heart of the ring of the rise where the fish might have nibbled, what, five, six seconds before? You think a fish will jump for the same bait twice? No sort of fish you'd want to hook.

Don't cast to the rise, cast around it, cast far and wide, cast just to the side where the fish might meander believing he's getting a second chance, a second unsuspecting fly, believing the first fly got away. He'll be more grateful, more determined second time round.

Don't cast to the rise, cast into one of the consequent circles which radiate from the leap, echoing wider and wider till they all dissolve, indistinguishable, into the anonymous ripples on the back of the lake.

Parmachene Belle, fluorescent blue and orange like the eyeshade and lipstick of a girl in from the Styx, River of Hatred, flowing through Arcadia, whose waters dissolve any vessel they touch. Seventh stream of Hades, strangling like a python.

Those country girls are grateful for any adventure; suckers for an off-chance, they'll take any odds. I know, I have been there. Nights under neon in the high-school washroom, the flickering bare bulb of the local hotel ladies.

Polishing the orange, touching up the blue, checking the flash and strut before launching out again, casting to the rise, softly disguising with wide eyes and giggles, with silence and blushes, the hook which you're waiting to lodge in his gills.

My Parmachene Belle, vulgar naivety, who'd have believed you'd be the high rod? Champion trout tickler. Catch of the night. Mata Hari of the waters. It simply takes faith. And a quick, heavy priest.

13 Secrets: Love and Death

Yes, all right, I'll admit it. He played *Un Homme et Une Femme* that first night when he was driving me home. *Un Homme et Une Femme*. And, yes, I am a sucker for all that: the film, the music, Anouk Aimée, even the driver whose name I've forgotten. And the walks along the deserted winter beach somewhere in Northern France. And racing the train back to Paris in the rain. And above all the words. The promise of love. The dusky-voiced woman caressing the samba: *l'amour est bien plus fort que nous*.

Even when you know it isn't true you sit in the solid embrace of the car's seat, the engine vibrating beneath you, the dark, the speed, the heat, the stranger beside you. The song becomes a message, a promise.

He could have played Paul Simon; he's about that age, that generation, in his late forties now, maybe early fifties – somewhere between Elvis and the Beatles, stuck in Graceland: losing love is like a window in your heart.
Or Monteverdi's *Vespers;* he could have played the *Vespers* and talked about the humanity of John Eliot Gardiner's interpretation.
Or Madonna: he could have played *Dick Tracy,* Dickdickdickdick, to establish the atmosphere.
He could have played Tom Waits – those California tangos celebrating urban sleaze, the low croon, the guitar; the mood would have been almost the same.
But not quite.

Puisque je vous aime . . . There's always the hope, somewhere hovering, curled like fiddleheads under the snow. Waiting. Against all the odds – nature as gambler –

for the six feet of snow frozen over their heads to dissolve. And the miracle is that it does. Spring comes and the fiddleheads unfurl into ferns which grow into roadside weeds with the heat. And by autumn they're curling back again, the edges dry and brown, crumbling back into the earth to endure another winter, to wait for another spring.

That hope of . . . call it 'love', for want of a more precise word. The Eskimos have twenty-nine words for snow. They say. They say the Persians have five words for fart. The Dutch have a word for the holes in the ice that unsuspecting skaters slip into, to be sucked away by the current, under the smothering blanket of the lake's solid ceiling. All the degrees of precision in speech, and we only have one word for love. I love that hat/ my cat/ ice-cream/ the sun/ the new weatherman on the telly/ my father/ husband/ son. She loved him to death. He died of unrequited love. Don't you love the way men cringe when you talk of castration? Love.

Always the expectation; the blind, bizarre, irrational, optimistic hope of love.

So, yes, he played the tape which meant we didn't need to talk. Another mistake. It means you fill the silence with your fantasies of who he is.

It turns out. Well, he's into God. He's into sitting side by side on the sofa holding hands and listening to samba/ tango/jazz. I'm too controlled for improvised jazz; the stuff puts me to sleep. It reminds me of the endless camomile afternoons of my childhood when Mother was making strawberry jam and there was nothing to do but listen to the crickets or dodge the lines of swallow shit from the telephone wires where the swallows sat from dawn to dusk, doing . . . who knows what? The gossip squad.

Me, I like a beat I can anticipate, a structure I can push against.

Spontaneity is fine in bed but on the dance floor you need rules. Rules. Yes, of course he dances, but I don't think he believes in sex before marriage. *Un Homme et Une*

Femme, sitting in a flat in Camberwell, an apartment in the ghetto, a room in some Vermont village over the local post office drinking Celestial Seasonings' Almond Sunset Tea. Samba/tango/jazz. And God.

'Jazz' means 'sex', I tell him. The word evolved in the brothels of Harlem, I tell him, attempting to plant the seed of an idea. It was deemed too racy to be used in polite society.

And tango? he asks.

Tango might be the name of an African instrument. The tango combines the beat of the black slaves with the rhythms of the Catholic slave owners. The tango began in the suburbs, the abattoirs, the docklands. It was a man's dance to begin with, men as roosters, cocks if you like: the metaphors of battle – men as peacocks, strutting their stuff. They'd practise with each other before moving into the brothels. Only the hookers, only the whores would dance the tango; it was too wild for decent women.

But, I hurry to assure him, the dance went to Paris with Carlos Gardel; that's where it became fashionable. The pope tried to ban it but only succeeded in guaranteeing its popularity. The version which returned to Buenos Aires was quite tame, so everybody dances it now. Shall we? Do you tango?
(It takes two . . .)
He doesn't. He just likes the music.

'And samba?' he asks when I move to go. This I don't know. I debate bluffing it, bullshitting him, but just in case his God is real I hold back and admit it: I don't know.
And you don't much care for jazz, do you? He guessed it. He saw the far-away horizons in my eyes.

We only had the one date. But I bought the tape after that for myself.

Dear Mum: I lost the pearl necklace you gave me on my sixteenth birthday. Yes, I know it belonged to Gran, your mother, and her mother before her. Yes, I know you wanted me to pass it on to my children, your grandchildren. Perhaps there won't be any offspring anyway. I didn't know whether to tell you. I never know how much to say: to you, to anybody.

Once I went out with a med student who told me how to commit suicide. Simple steps that anyone could follow. Straightforward household items. It's the techniques that count, more than the ingredients. At the time I asked him, quite innocently, as we walked along the tow path, as the rowers fought the river's muscle with their own sinewy arms, as the horses pulled their gaudy barges, all gypsy-red with bright blue poppies painted on the sides, as we strolled along the Cherwell to the Perch or the Trout or any one of several drinking places, I asked him what he'd learned that day. He said he'd learned how to commit suicide.

Oh, I said; and how do you do that?

He replied he couldn't say: 'Professional ethics.'

He had integrity, he genuinely thought he wouldn't tell me. But I knew he would. The knowledge was too great to keep.

So simple. It's one of those things – like sex, or the fact that Adam and Eve are a myth – it's so simple you can't believe you didn't already know it.

Perhaps you did.

I can't tell you, of course; he swore me to secrecy.

Perhaps I will tell you before we separate.

Perhaps I'll put it down in code.

Perhaps I already have.

Once I told another lover: I passed on the secret. Chinese whispers. One night in bed, early on when we were still exchanging secrets, swapping versions of each other's lives, recreating our pasts, this for that, tit for tat. I noticed that he had two tiny marks across his wrist. Suicide, I thought. Though he didn't seem the type. He didn't seem profound enough for such despair. He didn't seem active enough to bother to succumb. Boredom: yes. Depression: perhaps. But I wouldn't have thought he was capable of such a permanent commitment.

What's this? I muttered casually, tracing my finger across his wrist, his tiny scars like four little insects, bees, bee bites.

'Nothing.'

Tell me, I said. Did you cut your wrists?

'I'll never tell.'

Tell me! I bit him.

'No.' His eyes blazed.

Why not? I won't mind. I bent my head over his hands and licked his wrist. I slid my tongue along the tiny groove.

'I'm allowed to keep some things to myself. You know everything else about me. I'll tell you some other time.'

This is the problem with secrets.

If you loved me you'd tell, I tried to cajole him.

'If you loved me you wouldn't ask.'

I'll do anything.

'No.'

I jumped on him. I tickled him. I unbuttoned his shirt and licked his chest, nipped at the hairs around his breasts, bit his nipples.

You can do anything you like to me, I murmured. You can tie me up.

'I can tie you up anyway.'

Yes, but I won't scream. I will scream. I'll do anything you want me to, just TELL ME!

'No. It's my secret.'

Red rag.

I'll tell you a secret . . . I tried a different tack. I'll tell you how to commit suicide.

'Anyone can commit suicide: jump out of a window, slit your wrists, drink a bottle of Harpic.'

But what if it fails? I taunted. What if you end up with a broken spine? Or you're found in the bath and put into a nut house? Or the Harpic burns so much that you stop when you're brain damaged or blinded or speechless but still alive? That's what happens to most aspiring suicides: they botch it up and then they're watched for the rest of their lives so they never get the chance to do it properly.

A shadow of hesitation flickered across his face.

I can tell you how to do it painlessly, how to do it successfully, first time, in one smooth, easy formula.

He paused. I had him. 'How?' he muttered.

First you tell me what happened to your wrist.

'No, first you tell.'

No, you go first.

'You go.'

So I told him.

Then he told me.

He hadn't slit his wrists; the scars were the result of an operation to get some veins for his heart or his hips or something. And yes, he was right to hold out. As soon as I knew, I knew I'd been right all along: he wasn't the sort to commit suicide, he hadn't the passion, the depth, the despair. But by then he had my secret.

Later, when I negotiated a restructuring of the relationship which he could see was another way of splitting up, that night, the night I said, we need some space or I do anyway even if you don't, that night as I was drifting off to sleep, he recited to me those three easy steps, the foolproof guide to suicide.

Bastard.

Bastard! I shouted; you're blackmailing me.

'You told it to me,' he whispered.

It's your responsibility now. I simply gave you the knowledge, it's up to you what you do with it.

'That's what Nobel said about his dynamite. That's what Oppenheimer said about his bomb.'

Fuck off, I muttered, rolling away from him.

The sex we had that night was the best ever. I thought he was going to murder me. Murder me or kill himself. But we both survived. I think he did. Last time I heard, he was still alive.

Secrets, secrets; she knew about secrets. Small town life is full of secrets: black bags dumped in ditches, leaking things you wouldn't want to know. The doctor, the cop, the undertaker, all know the secrets. Hatch 'em, match 'em and dispatch 'em. And the hairdresser. And the pharmacist. And the librarian.

The librarian knew about the man who sat at the tiny tables in the children's stacks every Monday underlining the dirty words: bum, bottom, breast, burp. Sometimes he tore out pictures of girls. The librarian couldn't prove it was him. The board thought she was over-reacting. In truth they thought she was a little hysterical because she lived alone. The board decided they had a civic obligation to the man; there was nowhere else for him to go on Mondays when his mother did her day at the hospital kitchen. Sixty-eight years old, it was a crime a woman her age . . . But what could anyone do? She needed the money. And perhaps her day away from him was a relief of sorts.

The man and his mother lived in one of the tumbled-down houses beyond the gravel pit. His mother never had a husband; some said her father was his father as well.

It wasn't until the girls were snatched that they finally put him away. One summer – it must have been in the early sixties when everybody had long blond hair – two girls swimming at the gravel pit were abducted. They didn't see the man, he put black bags over their heads and bundled them into the woods. They were found at dusk with their hair shorn off, crying by the side of the road.

Nobody proved it was done by the man, but after they locked him up the books in the library stopped being defaced.
A few months later the man's mother died.

In the dark basement of the community centre candles flicker valiantly, trying to create intimacy while in fact simply reinforcing the gloom. We bump and bob against each other, the women in dungarees, the women in Doc Martens, the odd aspiring bluestocking dressed in the costume of Vita and Virginia: a badly-cut jacket, a long tweedy skirt.

'She went on and on about her gonorrhoea,' the woman beside me spits; 'gonorrhoea, gonorrhoea, all she could talk about all evening was her fucking gonorrhoea, then she has the nerve to say that it's a secret.'

And later, several hours into the night, brushing past her in my passage to the exit, 'I mean, who wants to spend a whole evening hearing about somebody's gonorrhoea?'

Effra, Falcon, Graveney, Quaggy, Tyburn, Walbrook, Wandle, Fleet.

I have been thinking about drowning recently. I can't get the idea out of my head. I'm convinced the cable will snap and we'll all plunge into the boiling sea at the centre of the earth.

Or a flood will break out and all the exits will be blocked: 'Delay due to London Fire Brigade.' Fire? Water? I'll be stuck on the platform as the trains race through with faces pressed against the glass, staring out at me, hands raised, fingers smearing, teasing, taunting. So close. So clear I can even make out the prints, the fingerprints penetrating my brain, but it doesn't matter since the trains don't stop so I'll never trace them anyway.

Sometimes the trains stop but the doors don't open. Water flows, licking my feet, rising to my knees, my thighs, up to my chin, my mouth, my nose, my ears. I know the train is there, I can smell its diesel smell, I can feel its hard shiny walls, I can just about hear it screeching and sighing to a halt before the water seeps in to fill my ears.

Death by drowning, by driving. I feel the impact, I anticipate it, I brace myself for the crash, easing onto the roundabout, crossing a road, cruising down a highway I prepare myself for the unexpected contact. Head on: the all-embracing smash.
I long to give over and end the anticipation.

And someone's cat is dying. And someone's father's dying. And someone's love affair is dying. The sun dies every evening, the daffodils die back each spring, the woman's anger is dying down, slowly, with time.

So few words for dying when it happens all around us.

J rings me from her bungalow in a small town at the edge of the prairies. It's Saturday afternoon my time. I've just come in from looking at flats. I seem to spend my whole life looking for a place to live. She's yawning at me down the line. It's early morning her time. She starts to talk about a poem she read last night in the *Atlantic*. She shuffles through the papers by her bed. I hear them rustle all the way across the ocean, across the continent.

I ask aimlessly about her sisters. What are they doing? They're all meeting up at her parents' on the Cape for a month in the summer: the kids, the dogs, the station wagons. Families.

Families.

Suddenly I burst into tears. It's the idea of people living in small towns. Getting on with their lives. It's the image of J still in bed, with her man looking after the kids 'cause it's Saturday morning, cooking breakfast: doughnuts or waffles or pancakes – kiddie treats – and huge plastic cartons of milk, overflowing, spilling everywhere.

'But darling, you didn't want it. You didn't want any part of it. You wouldn't touch it with a ten-foot pole.'

Yes I know.

'You've spent your whole life running as far away from all this as you possibly can.'

I always was the sort to cry over spilt milk.
And I still haven't found a place to live.
I always wanted to live by the ocean.
Oceans always scare me.
I always wanted to be the sort of person who lived by the ocean. I always seem to end up living beside rivers.

Suddenly spring comes and the streets are full of women: women with babies, pregnant women pushing babies in prams. Sunday brings them out in force.

I want I want I want a child.

You would, now it's too late.
You had your chance when you were married.
Now you'll never get another chance again.

I want to waddle heavy and languid.
I want to wallow.
I want to be a ball of flesh in Madonna dresses.
I want to billow like a balloon.
I want to soak up the sun like a stone, like a sponge, like a buttercup bursting.
I want to be fat with the earth.
I want to feel a child snuffling at my breast, stirring the veins and the arteries, sucking right down to the roots of this tree.

You've got to stop seeing your life as a movie with you in the starring role. Until you start taking things seriously you never will get anywhere.

The audience is there, sure; watching, waiting for the next instalment. But they don't really care. It's an evening's entertainment for them, like *Dallas* or *Dynasty*. They switch off at the end of the episode then lock the back door and flick off the lights and climb with weary contentment up the stairs, to the neat little bedroom, into the bed made with tight, impenetrable hospital corners. They climb between their fresh, pressed sheets, with their clean, white partners and dream their technicolour dreams, leaving you alone in the dark.

It isn't worth it, this life you are leading, simply to amuse your friends. Amuse. A muse.

Beware, you may get addicted to this life.

You see him staring at you across the room. He's caught you looking at him. He crosses the space, towers over you, looking down.

Why did you approach me? you ask a little later.

'Because you looked like someone who was looking for someone to share their life with.'

Is it real? Is it fantasy? These looks across a room: does anyone really believe in them? And yet there he is beside you, in your room, your bed. And of course these things end as abruptly as they began, although all along you believed this would be The One. And perhaps it could have been. Or perhaps there isn't One at all. Perhaps One doesn't exist for you, for anybody.

I never had the man in the dirty raincoat paying in popcorn or sticky sweets to run his hand beneath my skirts in cinemas – or in my case the Co-op building by the bridge. But I've read the story so often I feel the violation is my own. The reward, the guilt. The unspoken bargain.

It happened in late adolescence, working in the library one night I felt the mellowing swell of warm air between my thighs. Without thinking I moved forward, spreading out, opening up, giving myself over to the heat until the question penetrated: why? And looking down I saw a man crouched beneath the table, his wide eyes staring white at me from the darkness below. I jumped, released a soundless cry, slammed my books and hurried off.

Why didn't I kick, scream, expose the man?
Was it simply surprise?
Was it complicity?

And now, of course, I wonder what he would have done had I remained. This question has insinuated itself into the episode, has grafted itself upon the story, titillating speculation: the stranger who will service one then disappear. The faceless man.

This is not a fantasy of rape, this search for the *acte gratuit*, the union without responsibilities, without repercussions, the zipless fuck.

It must have seemed quite possible in those bath houses ten, fifteen years ago. The moist fingers dripping from the walls, the arms reaching from dark corners, the straps and chains and intricate contraptions: a playground, a cavern, an adventure café. A perfect fantasy, because at the end of the night we can turn on the lights and all go home to sleep. Dreaming of the wrist, the thigh, the sudden sweep of translucent skin like a scarf of silk, a suddenly trembling fritillary beneath one's coarse, demanding hands.

I have a friend who claims that gay men have it right. Queers/Queens/Faggots/Pansies/Nancy Boys live out the life that we straights simply dream of. Casual sex: the pick-up in the Tuileries, the Bois de Boulogne, behind the Spaniard's Inn, in the heart of the Heath, beneath the cross at the top of Mount Royal, in the bath houses, the bookshops, the foyers of certain theatres that somehow everybody seems to know about.

The flash of an eye. The odd word. A cigarette. A quick dip into the shadows. A grunt, a groan, a whimper, and then they are gone.

Is this the ideal? Is this how it will be when the structures dissolve and psychopaths rule? A quick grope in a black hole then a candlelight dinner with friends – men or women. To curl in front of the telly then wander up to bed. Alone.

To stretch into each of the corners, to snore and fart and eat biscuits, to let the crumbs scratch your back like a geisha, the tiny skirt still tingling, the bud still pulsating from the secret post- or pre-prandial encounter in the dark.

Love? It doesn't only happen when you're open to it, only when there are holes, only when something is missing. No, that's not the way. Sometimes you can be so full, full as a nut, as a fat balloon floating above the river, as a polka-dot on a silk dress, so content, so bursting with it all, with with with . . . happiness.

People see that. They feel it. They want a part of it. And when you're so full, you want to share it. And some days you're afraid you will burst. Some days everything seems good, seems possible, seems all right. So you do, you answer the call. People respond to a need. So you, yes you do try to help, you open up, you open yourself, you try to give some of it away, to spread it around, to share it too. That's all. And then, that's it. It begins. The rot, the trouble, the terrible seeping sway. Invisibly, imperceptibly. One day it's all all right and the next it has begun to die.

14 What To Wear

What does one wear to a seduction? A possible seduction. A date. Clean underwear, of course, new perhaps, but not silk, not silk satin, not a black suspender belt. Not the first time. You don't want to look like you expected to end up undressing together; you don't want him to think this is normal, this underwear is normal for you; then he might take you for a tart. So you put on your best, whitest, M & S knickers and matching bra: low-cut, with lace.

The key layer is the next one. The green dress brings good luck, but you already wore it, that party you met. Jeans? Too studenty: 'Hard, cold, angry', your husband used to say. Say something often enough, you believe it. Am I hard? Do I destroy? Better choose something soft, warm: flowing dress, flower-sprigged, unthreatening. Is the colour too insipid? Bright blues. Moody blues. Lapis.

Now the legs: tights in a ball by the ankles, knotted round the knees. Tights are a bad bet for seduction. Crotch rot. What's the alternative? Stay-ups: flesh bulging out the tops, leaving elastic marks round the thighs: if you do it in lamplight he might think you have some disease, contagious, a pox on the skin. Or sox like a little girl? Mutton as lamb. Bare legs: long white slugs. Shave them, being careful to catch the collar of hairs round the ankle, the give-away ring.

Jewellery? No rings – too poignant. Bracelets clatter on the table. The pearl necklace gets caught up if you try kissing. Brooch? Old-lady jewellery; besides, it might come unstuck and get lost.

Fun, they say: 'Have fun.' I haven't had fun in a relationship since I was twelve. Some say it's much easier being single: neglected, you can neglect yourself. Being single you have to take so much more care. Since I left R again I'm exhausted. Permanently exhausted these days. I only realized how exhausted when I noticed my eyes. Red. Always red.

I suppose I didn't get to bed until three-thirty, four o'clock last night. You forget these things, the luxuries of being single. It was a date. A date: funny, old-fashioned word. I could have slept with the guy. I was sitting in the cinema thinking: I could sleep with him. I could feel the heat rising from his thigh next to mine. I crossed my legs, he crossed his. We were in tune with each other. The film was lousy, though that didn't matter.

But later in the car – I drove him home – that's the difference: grown-up dates – it's easier, you're in control. We sat in the car. Talking. His ex, my ex. Past relationships. I kept thinking, I could sleep with him, but by then I was tired. Also I hate waking up in someone else's bed. So when he finally invited me in I said it was too late.

I got home at about two-fifteen; there were eight messages on the machine. R doesn't leave messages; he rings and hangs up. I know because sometimes I filter my calls. He rings to see if I'm there; if I'm not he hangs up so I won't know he called. The eight messages were all from my husband. My ex. My soon-to-be ex-husband. He has this extraordinary ability to know when I'm out with a new man. Weeks go by without a word but the one night I've got a date is the night he invariably rings.

We had, it must be admitted, met earlier in the day, but that in itself is rare enough.

1. 'Hi. It's four o'clock. Fancy a drink tonight?'
2. 'I'm leaving the office now; I'll be in the pub.'
3. 'It's me; I'm in the pub.'
4. 'Hi, I've left the pub, just to let you know, I'm home.'

5. 'Walking the dog. Back in five minutes. Give me a ring.'
6. 'It's midnight; give me a ring.'
7. 'It's me. It's two in the morning.'
8. 'It's two-fourteen; ring me; don't worry about waking me.'

So I did. I mean, I don't hate the guy and he was waiting. We'd had a fight that morning. I'd gone to borrow the hoover. I told him the place was a tip, a shit heap. It was. The place was dying, dying of neglect, I said. No, call it abuse, not neglect. I said, it's dying of abuse. I keep telling him. It doesn't matter; it's not my place anymore, but it does make me sad. But it's not my problem anymore. I've told him before. He says I only see the worst.

It's a shitheap, I said.

'It isn't; you always say that.'

So I showed him. I just pointed: the phone books spread across the shelves. The unopened mail spilling everywhere so you can't even see the tablecloth beneath it. The clothes piled all over the place, not even stuck in corners, in little piles all over the floor. I didn't say a thing; I simply pointed.

He grabbed my head, my ears I suppose, one ear and a hunk of hair on the other side. Occasionally he does that; he loses it. This calm, quiet, dignified, this polite, dark-blue pinstriped man . . . Quite suddenly he blows. Goes berserk. When he used to do it I'd think: he's going to kill me. Like when he drove too fast on the highway, or overtook on a curve, or pulled into the oncoming lane to pass a line of traffic I used to think, I'll be damned if I'm going to say no or don't or stop or slow down. I thought it again this time.

He grabbed my head and shook it and I knew he wanted to smash it open. If I'd been up against a wall he'd have smashed my head against it. I knew it, but I wasn't scared. I never am when he gets like this. I go strangely calm. I don't really mind it: at least it's a response, a reaction. In the absence of everything else, at least it's passion, of a sort. 'Passion', like 'patient' or 'patience'.

From the Latin 'suffering', the word evolved to mean 'pain' . . . and all the other contemporary variations.

This violence. This rage. These rare eruptions I can understand.

He was shaking my head, he was shouting: 'It isn't a tip, it isn't a tip!' Pulling my hair, crushing my ear; he could have killed me but all I could think of was my earring. I was afraid he'd rip it out of my ear. It was a silver and lapis earring I'd bought from the Berbers in Marrakesh.

I listened for the earring, I strained to hear it falling.
I thought: I mustn't lose the little butterfly bit at the back; if I lose that bit the earring's useless.

That's what I was thinking, even though I knew he was trying to smash my head open, I was thinking about him accidentally ripping the thing out of my ear.
I was thinking: I wonder if the ear has blood, if it bleeds when it's ripped open? I don't think it does. At least it won't stain the carpet, I thought.

Then suddenly he stopped. Just stopped. Still. Silence. We stared at each other a moment then I noticed the wastepaper basket, tipped over onto the floor: paper, wrappers, apple cores spread across the carpet. I pointed to it.
A tip, I muttered. Then I walked away.

He was still staring at it when I closed the door.

That's why he had rung, though he didn't mention the fight at all. I called him back. Hi, I said, it's me.
He said, did I want to come round? He didn't ask where I'd been, who with.
I said, it's two-twenty in the morning.
He said, he was already in bed or he'd come up to me.
I said, by the time I get there you'll be asleep.
He said he wouldn't.
What else could I do? People respond to a need. I got back in the car and went round.

He'd cleaned the place up: the clothes, the mail, the telephone books. All gone. He didn't say a thing about it, the mess, the fight, the grand clean up. He just let me in and we went up to bed.

Victory? This is victory, of a sort, for me. For him, if not defeat, at least it is a concession. All those years together and it isn't till we separate that we can reach this harmony. The violence is rare. More frequently it comes from me: the time I threw the teapot, the time I thrust his fist through the window. I don't really think we'll kill each other: such long odds, a tiny risk, gamble, like everything else. If one of us did it would be chance, an accident, a gesture we'd both colluded in. Like me conceding on the wall-to-wall or him agreeing to go for red. Carpets. Curtains. The battle-ground still shows the stains. The clock ticks on.

By then it must have been three, three-thirty. By the time I fell asleep it must have been closer to four.

Will I go back to him? I don't know. The older you get the more difficult it is to imagine yourself with somebody new. The dog was sleeping so deeply, snoring away at the foot of the bed. With these red eyes, am I likely to find someone else anyway? It's just that I'm always so tired. So bone-tired. So exhausted. So sick of all the fighting. So sick of starting out again.

You must learn to release the past. You mustn't let it entangle you, weigh you down, swallow you up. You must learn to let go of things before they pull you under.

15 Madelaine/Marina

I think I fell in love with their pasts as much as with their presents. All the lonely childhoods, all the tortured adolescents, all the perfect lovers. It was their lovers I fell in love with. I first noticed R when he told me about Madelaine. All his lovers before me were called Mary or Marie or Marina or some variation on the Virgin/Whore. And yes, his mother died when he was still a child.

Madelaine: she was the one, the real love of his life. Of course. They met at Harvard or MIT. She was Irish I think, moved in with an ex-girlfriend of R's after college. They were all good friends, used to rent cabins in the Laurentians, go cross-country skiing for long weekends between terms. Her companion joined the diplomatic corps and they moved away while R was still writing his thesis. During his holidays he would visit them in Zagreb and Nairobi – wherever they were posted.

She had so much of him, his poems. He was never much good, he claimed, but he loved poetry. He studied it, read it, composed it and even took a writing course one year, he admitted, blushing profusely, an evening course. He told me this the first time I was in his study: those huge high walls, that mansion-block Gothic; the study had once been a bedroom in the days when flats like his would have had servants living in. What surprised me was the rows of thin little poetry books stacked like toy soldiers against the grey walls. Poetry. I never would have thought it of him.

But when I asked to see some of his poems he said he'd given them all to a friend. To her, I later realized: to Madelaine. She was moving to Rio or Jakarta or some such place and wanted something to read on the plane. I asked why he hadn't continued to write after that. He'd lost the urge, he said. I suppose he didn't need to. I suppose he learned to write poetry for her and once she had his offerings he didn't need to write anymore.

Another time we were talking about wine – Marsala or Madeira. He said he'd first encountered it at breakfast one morning on the terrace of her apartment in Toulouse. They served fresh orange juice from the tree in the garden, and Marsala, and croissants.

At the time he was a lowly lecturer in some crummy small-town university and it seemed so sophisticated, 'The height of sophistication,' he said at the time. It still does to me.

What did she do with her days? I wanted to know. I wanted her to be unproductive: a housewife, a kept woman, a woman I could have contempt for. At the same time I also wanted her to do something exotic: restore paintings, collect icons, research medieval saints or something. As much as I wanted to diminish her, I also wanted her to be as perfect as he thought she was.

It turns out she taught astronomy. 'In Toulouse?' I asked. 'In French?' This was too much: the recipient of his only poems, a sipper of Marsala in the mornings, and an astronomer to boot! And in French! And on top of all that she was also mothering her children. She adopted seven Vietnamese babies. They would be almost my age, he smiled. He was twenty years older than me.

'Thinking about it now,' he mused, 'her children would be just about as old as you are now.' I wondered if she had a son.

They used to travel together, she and R. He'd arrive from Akron or Toledo or one of those dinky little Midwest towns, to wherever they were living – Barcelona or Mombasa. And her companion would be busy being diplomatic, so she and R would travel down to the sea or up to the mountains or into the interior.

Once he told me that he'd never actually slept with her. Another time he said they'd shared a bed. Another time he said they'd slept together once, on safari in Kenya. It had been a mistake, he said. Another time he said, yes, of course they had made love on these journeys, but it was casual, easy. He was sure her partner knew and didn't care. Her partner was a woman. Did I mention that already? They were a very cosmopolitan couple. And you mustn't forget, all this took place in the sixties.

Once he described how he and Madelaine had driven all the way from Paris to Budapest in the middle of the night to attend the final performance of a little-known Verdi opera. Driving over cobblestones into the city just waking at dawn. They'd checked in to this old château – if that's what they're called in Hungary – an old stone castle on the river.

I'd like to go to Budapest some day, I murmured, prompting him to continue. He didn't reply. He didn't continue the story.
Why don't you get the poems back from her? I suggested; I'd like to read them too.
'She's dead,' he said. 'She died five years ago.'
The best ones always do.

Marina lived in a sixth-floor walk-up on one of those grotty little dead ends leading off the harbour in Marseilles, full of Arab restaurants and dirty little grocery shops, full of pastries bruised by flies fresh from the dog shit in the gutter, full of dusty dented tins of things with Arab writing on them.

I never actually met Marina but R and I stayed in her flat once when we were travelling through Marseilles on our way back from Bastia or Algeria or one of those awful places he used to have to go to. He said he was a business consultant teaching Third-World governments how to trade with the affluent West. I think in fact he was a spy.

When I first proposed the theory he just smiled. Come to think of it, in all the years I've known him he has never actually denied it.

Marina's flat was tiny and cramped and carved out of several attic spaces. There were only two windows in the whole place. From the sitting room you could look out over a choppy sea of sloping roofs to the harbour beyond. When the sun went down the roofs turned from copper green through pink to grey: the colours of the pigeons who used to nestle in the eaves, cooing like the waves on a calm ocean evening.

Her kitchen was the only other room in the flat with a window, if you could call it that. It opened onto the stone wall of a building an arm's length away. Fresh air? No. It only acted as a flue, conducting into her tiny kitchen the greasy kebab smells from the street below. I wondered why they bothered poking a hole in the wall at all, but R said when he lived there twenty years before it was a separate flat.

Apparently an old Arab woman lived with her young lover in what had become Marina's kitchen. It could have been her son, I suggested. The place was no more than six feet square; a small dog cage is larger. 'Nope,' R assured me, 'if you'd heard the noises I used to hear through the walls you'd know they were lovers.' I had to give him that; the walls were tinder-dry and thin as ricepaper. In a fire they'd have all gone up: Marina and R, the wrinkled old Arab and her gingery lover.

Even with the added kitchen, Marina's flat seemed impossibly small for a human being to inhabit. The bedroom was a wall around the bed with just a curtain separating it from the rest of the flat. The bedroom was, in fact, the bed. The bathroom had a cold-water tap. The sitting room was supported, wall to wall, with books. Dotted along the shelves were the vacant-eyed stares of Victorian dolls with yellowing lace hats and waxy faces. Some were huge fat babies. Others were scrawny thin young women. If I'd ever been disposed to like Marina these dolls would have turned me against her.

'Why do you have to use her name?' R will ask when he reads this. 'Why can't you disguise the place, the people? She'll recognize herself. She'll hate me for it,' he'll protest.

Why should I bother? Marina as she is is better than any fictionalization of Marina.

And why should I care if she hates him – or me – for mentioning her? She always hated me. Did I say we didn't meet? Well, in fact, we did. Just once. In her flat. She was dressed like a Colette heroine: black pleated skirt, white ruffled shirt, dressed like a sixteen-year-old ingénue, though she must have been at least fifty by then.

Before we met, when I still had only R's stories to go on, I expected to fall in love with Marina. She was single then, 'between lovers'. She seemed to spend most of her life between lovers. A student of Derrida. A Wittgenstein scholar. A patient of Lacan. Names I knew of, knew I should know about, but didn't. So many gaps.

Still, she called herself a feminist but she ignored me the whole afternoon I was there.

I remember noticing stacks of tinned oysters stored in Marina's kitchen cupboard. Oysters were once the food of peasants. Hardly surprising, living in shallows, feeding on sewage: globs of phlegm washed down with champagne . . . If they weren't so rare now nobody would dream of eating them.

But she didn't feed us the oysters that afternoon, she fed us canned stew and rice for lunch: a French woman, living over a market, and she fed us canned meat stew. She'd already eaten when we arrived, although we were invited for lunch. I was expecting fresh fish from the harbour, and pâté and baguette and bitter green salad and she fed us from one of those dusty Arab cans . . . And her a Jew.

R insisted they'd never been lovers, but it was clear, watching her, that they had. Or if they hadn't she wished they had. Or else she flirted with every man. She was one of those women who hate other women. Male-directed.

I suppose what I loved in R was his versions of the women he loved. And the ones he loved most were the ones he never had, the ones who died or who rejected him. That's why he will always love me, because I will always leave him.

Although I only met her once, I found that over the next few months I began to dream about Marina. It was a recurring dream. I dreamed I'd gone to interview her. Everyone was sitting in a courtyard at a long table eating and drinking. They were all ignoring me. I couldn't understand why all these strangers were ignoring me. When the meal ended they all drifted off back to Paris in their Renaults and Citroens and Deux Chevaux, and I realized that we were in a village in the country and I wondered if I'd have trouble getting back.

When the last guest had left and I was alone with Marina I realized that they all assumed I was her lover. What's more, she knew this and let them think it, which is why no one had offered me a lift. There I was, trapped, alone with R's Marina, in her house in the French countryside . . .

Sometimes the dream ended with me entering the courtyard, seeing all the people, the sweating *pichets* of wine, the circles of brie, the chunks of *chèvre*, the crumb-strewn wooden table, the baskets overflowing with yellow pears and pink apricots. Sometimes I got to the point where I wondered why nobody was speaking to me, where I wondered how I would get home, where I wondered when I would finally get to interview her. After I realized I was alone with her I don't know what happened next. Perhaps that's where the dream ended. Perhaps that's as far as the dream ever went. Or perhaps something else occurred that I've forgotten.

The mind blocks what it can't admit.

R drifting off to sleep: 'We can't go on like this; we have to make a decision. Quick: the water's rising up to meet us, we have to decide which way to turn.'

Who is we? I ask gently, hoping to reach right into the dream.
'I don't know,' he answers, waking.

He describes being at the top of a hill, looking down at the road. The river which runs across it is flooding.

'With you I feel more myself than I ever have.'
'I can say anything; I can ask you anything . . .'

He talks on and on, preoccupied with sex, with death – how odd, stupid it all is, with love.

'I can't bear it, I'm going to lose you. I'll lose you tomorrow,' he moans, meaning, 'I'll lose you forever.'
He wants me to contradict him. He wants me to say, don't be ridiculous; you'll have me again next week, next month . . .

But I don't contradict him. I know it is true. I've already left him. I left him the moment we met at that party in the garden, years and years ago.

Then in the morning, first thing on waking: 'I talk such rot at night before sleeping; don't take any notice of what I say . . .'

R says, one day just before we part. Again.
We part. I part. We meet again. We part.
R is my anchor. He senses I'm about to make another voyage.

He says – for his own pride perhaps, or is he telling me that this is the final docking in his port? he says: anyone would be mad to get involved with you now; now you've bled your marriage all over the streets.

He says – perhaps it's true – he says my husband is the only man I'll ever really love, because he's the only man who's ever really left me. Did he jump? Was he pushed? R doesn't know about the late-night visits to my husband.

He says: I wouldn't ever buy you a ring; I know what you would do with it.

He says: you're like some sugar doll; when the sun is out you're clear and cold and solid as a rock, but as soon as it starts to rain you dissolve like a sandcastle in the path of an incoming tide.

16 Exiles

Winds flow from west to east carrying the heat, the dirt, the stink of tanneries and slaughterhouses, the sulphur of the paper mills and sewage plants. The lucky ones move east to west pursuing cleaner air. She moved widdershins, travelling backwards to old lands.

Write about your past, they say; write about your own history. Write about what you know, where you come from, who you are. The way forward is the way back: it's one of those phrases which floats around.

The stories one hears: headless bodies on the beaches; boys in sleeping bags, their heads exchanged; hundreds of dollars in travellers' cheques still stashed in their backpacks; it's just for fun.

These foreigners . . . What can you say? White women's flesh to a foreigner . . .

'I've been on this highway almost six hours already and nobody's offered me a lift.'

'Come to dinner next Tuesday,' the machine demanded, 'and bring your mystery man; we're dying of curiosity.'
I will come, but I'll come alone.
'Oh no, it's your new man we want to see.'

The responsibility of being the storyteller.
I will tell the stories; I will not perform them.

'You're very secretive,' the machine accuses. 'You don't want him to meet your friends? We'll be best behaved. We won't make 'in'-jokes. We'll keep off religion and politics. What is he, a lefty, your new man? We'll gag our fascist friends.'

Oh, he can defend himself. But he'll suffocate in your swaddling chintz.

'Darling,' the machine exhales a mournful sigh, 'I do believe you're becoming a snob. Don't worry, we will stroke your peasant with kid gloves and drink from our saucers if that's what you want.'

Already I can hear the whispers: 'A bit of rough, a touch of the lash . . .'
Later, when I explain about the murder charge, they'll gasp and titter and slink home titillated by the secret knowledge that they almost/nearly/could easily have sat down to supper with a real live murderer.

I traversed America like Nancy Cunard with her black men her working men her rough men who were soft between the sheets, putting up in boxy rooms smelling of incontinence, in wooden beds whose tired embraces engulfed us like a swamp.

In the mornings tight-lipped women with fleshy arms peered through the curtains of their sagging bungalows till we departed.

'You go,' he'd say, 'you ask about a room, you do it so nice.' Then he'd follow when he heard the key plucked sullenly from its pigeon-hole.

Those were the nights when nothing could go wrong: the televisions were always too big, their pictures stretched and faded to diminish the distraction. The bars of soap were coffins to the totem hairs of the previous night's guests. The carpets, worn to rope, the undisguised warp and weft beside the bed, the telephone, the window looking onto a concrete parking lot, the bathroom; the four poles in the compass of those tiny rooms which were our world for six or twelve or eighteen hours out of every twenty-four.

Mo el/ H el/ otel. The Dew Drop Inn. The Bide A Wee. The Travellers' Friend. The Journey's End. All the neon mirages on the edges of roads which flow across the continent.

The arteries and veins, the blue roads and red roads. The highways and freeways. The turnpikes and paved roads and dirt roads and dead ends.

The faded checked shorts biting into blue-veined thighs, the blue jeans tucked into men's boots, but always with the promises: 'Cable TV/Water Bed/Unlimited Coffee'. The glimmer of suspicion as you pull into the drive. The thin eyes behind fat smiles: 'One night forty bucks. Coffee shop down the road is open at half past six.'

But each night as the door closed behind us the speculation ended until morning when they picked back their curtains counting the bodies out, anxious not to come across some shocking indiscretion.

'. . . Like, remember that time Rene found the woman tied to the bed smothered in her own puke? The man, he was a nice-looking fella. Always the ones. Carried a leather briefcase. We never even noticed the woman go in with him. Found him next evening. Drove his Chevy over a railway bridge into the river. Never found out if he was drunk or did it on purpose. Maybe he didn't even know about the woman. Maybe she was sleeping it off when he left. Maybe he slipped away while she snored, decided to let her sleep, poor wreck, not to wake her, just forgot to untie the ropes. Still it was a shock for poor Rene. Quit that morning. Went on welfare. Hasn't opened a bedroom door since. Well, it makes you think . . .'

Just before noon the rooms were cleaned; then they could all rest easy again until dark when the travellers started showing up again looking for sleep.

Those were the lives we invaded, me and my Russian just in from the Steppes. I'd met him in a taxi on the Upper

East Side. He had just arrived from Kamchatka – a name on the Monopoly board for me; for him it was home – no, home is not the place you leave. For him it was the place where he was born and raised.

Three days in Manhattan and already he was driving a big yellow taxi. Couldn't even say 'The Bronx'. He could say 'Have a nice day'. In America the taxi drivers never know their way around. I hailed him. We talked. I always was a sucker for an accent. Between Madison and East 18th it was all decided: we took a 'rent-a-wreck', took a 'rent-a-heap-cheap' across America. I wanted to see the other side; he wanted to see the world.

I left him with the car on the West Coast but he tracked me all the way to Notting Hill. He'd never have made it as an American although he tried. God knows, he tried. He learned his way around too well. And so he stayed with me for a few weeks before he disappeared again. To Paris, he said. He said he liked French choral music. I think he meant Piaf. I wonder if he knows that she is dead? Before he left he showed me how to get from Leicester Square to Chelsea in three minutes.

I never introduced him to my friends. When I explained about the murder charge they all said I was crazy to let him stay, and the machine stopped blinking its red eye.

I missed him when he went, I must confess. To be with a man whose language you don't speak: this is the easiest kind of companion.

After he'd gone I wondered, is it true? Am I a snob? It's simply easier not to try to introduce such people.
But is it?

The murder charge I twisted to convince them. Fairy stories.
Art is the lie that reveals the truth, Picasso said. My Russian was going off to Paris to visit artists' studios.

17 Hanging on / Hanging in

I read about her on a back page in the *New Yorker*. Alberta Hunter. She'd just come out of retirement, eighty-six or seven. She was appearing at this nightclub in the Village that some entrepreneur had established just for her. That name, Alberta: the sound of the prairies – lonely, long, the wind whistling over flat lands at dusk. It reminded me of a voice, her voice, I'd heard it on an old LP. So I dragged my man of the moment down to Washington Square and we sat in the murk of early evening as the place filled up with businessmen grabbing an extra g&t before dinner. I'd been told to come early if I wanted a seat.

My companion wasn't the sort to hang out in clubs. I don't think he appreciated the blues. He was pretty antsy by the time she appeared. This frail little bird of a woman. She'd been sitting at a table by the stage for most of the evening sipping a Coke. I'd noticed her, remarked on her, imagining she must be a fan from way back.

Then the canned music stopped. The compere announced, 'Alberta!' and this tiny little stick woman teetered to her feet. She had to be helped onto the stage by a waitress. You thought she wasn't going to make it, she was bound to croak before the first refrain was over. But as soon as the mike was placed in her hand she underwent a transformation.

Grey skin. Hair a thin twist of metallic threads tied in a knot at the top of her head. Face wrinkled as a walnut. Lips poppy red, caving inwards. In profile she stands like a little girl: belly thrust out, toes pigeoning in, grunting out her songs about men dragging women's hearts around, sassing and jazzing and whooping with the audience: gee but it's hard to love someone when that someone don't love you.

Down-hearted blues. Dead pan. Flirting with the audience. Feigning innocence: the innuendos firing like machine guns.

And just for a moment, arms akimbo in her sky-blue dress, she looks like . . . an angel. That beatific smile. That mischievous mouth. That serenity. That proclamation of good, of God: 'He is your only true friend, children listen to me, I'm old enough to know what it's all about, *'cause nobody knows you when you're down and out.'*

Then a quick, pink tongue darts and flicks across her lips. Her nose spreading in a pyramid across her face, nostrils flaring like the sphinx before Napoleon struck it off. No, this is no angel.

I side with the wives who hang on, who outlast their men, come hell or high water. Not for the money, no, nothing so brash; they outlast the airheads and the bimbos, the casual acquaintances, the passing obsessions, the respectable permanent mistresses. They outlive all the women and the Great Man for the glorious revenge of being the one to drop the first clod on his coffin.

Climbing out of retirement. Unseen for half a century. Everyone but the biographer had forgotten her existence. But there, on the day, squeezed into her black serge suit, her black straw hat, she suddenly appears from nowhere to lead the procession.

Mass. She comes forward. The common intake of breath as the family stares on in horror. The chorus of titters from the phalanx of journalists: which one is that? The mother? The sister? No, it's his wife. The wife! She's still alive? I thought the wife kicked off aeons ago . . . Do you suppose he knew? Do you suppose he communicated with her in his final . . . ?

She's come to exact the final twist of the knife, the prerogative of the widow. And as the dirt thuds on the hollow wood of the lid she thinks: finally, now, I too can die. And they all wonder whether she will carry her vengeance beyond the grave, decreeing her desire to lie beside him. We won't know yet, we won't know till she kicks it.

The spectre of his death seems to have revived the wife; she's seen all over Europe these days, cavorting around like some young goat. Nothing like a death in the family. New lease of life. I wish you long life, the Jews say when somebody dies. Though they were both Catholics. That was his tragedy; he was a convert. That was her triumph; she was born to it.

I must stop seeing men as the enemy. Old men. Oh yes, I am qualified to talk about old men. I'm becoming quite an expert in the field, a bit of a connoisseur: the rapist, the shrink, the father of my abortion, the lover, the one-night-stand . . .
And that's only the months since my husband and I separated.

This is the centre of the story, you see; this is the source of the flow.

When the child was five, in her blue polka-dot skirt with her new set of paints, sitting in a yellow field, an old man appeared beside her. He took a package from his pocket and pulled out a balloon. He blew it up and tied the end and gave it to her as a present. Then he took her hand and led her through the meadow.

They were looking for somebody, his wife or somebody, anybody. It was a game: they had to see if they could see somebody coming. She had to tell him if anybody came. Nobody came.

They went down the path beside the cemetery, through the poppy field, to a place by the river where there was a flat rock.

When it was over there was red mixed with the blue polka-dots in her skirt.

Just go to the river. Just get in, he said.

She was too afraid to tell him that she didn't know how to swim. He pushed her forward. Just stand in the river. It will all wash away. The river will wash it away. He said. Then he disappeared.

Acheron, River of Sorrows. Lethe, River of Forgetfulness. Cocytus, River of Lamentation. Phlegethon, River of Rage. Styx, River of Hate, conducting the shades into Hades.

The inky-black Styx, the fire-stream Phlegethon, the frozen Cocytus, the clear, sweet Lethe, the blue depths of the Acheron.

18 The Seine

I'm going, I said.
You're mad.
In the absence of passion one might as well seize adventure.
You don't even know the man, she replied.
So what? I will, by the time we get there. If nothing else it is an experience.
Why don't you stay home and work like the rest of us; you might get somewhere that way.
I have nothing to say. I'm empty. I'm dry.
If you don't put in the grind you'll never get anything finished.
There's bound to be a story in it; think of it as a working trip.

This is it. On this point I am adamant. One must not see one's life as a story, with a new chapter in each afternoon. One must not pillage one's life for something to write about. It is immoral. It is a dreadful way to live.

I'm going, I said. I went.

He picked me up at ten in the evening. We caught the midnight ferry, arrived at Calais when it was still dark. We drove all night, arriving in Paris just as dawn was breaking, cracking over the city like an egg.

I could hardly keep awake on the highway. I kept drifting off the highway, drifting off into sleep. But as we swung onto the peripherique with the sun sliding down the Eiffel Tower, slipping down the Seine . . .

'I love your book,' the note said. 'Please, come with me to Paris.'

I can't, I replied. I haven't got a nightgown.

That evening when I got home, waiting on my doorstep, wrapped in a white, silk satin gown, were a dozen blood-red roses with all their thorns removed, but one. We used it the next evening to pierce the full moon in the Seine.

When I returned the roses had died, but the thorn was still intact. I keep it upright in my shoe to remind me every morning how dangerous it is to be reflected in a river.

Ilia is the person with whom I explored perversities. I met him at an exhibition of Magnum photographs. I was taking notes before a photo of a Paris brothel. He started talking to me about it: the light, the aperture, the exposure. We talked about Brassai and Bresson. He referred to a book, offered to lend it to me, mentioned that he was going the next evening to Paris, to see an exhibition of work by a nineteenth-century photographer. A German baron, double-barrelled, Baron Something-Something; I've forgotten the name.

Over tea in the gallery café he explained that this baron used the young boys on a particular Greek island to pose in classical scenes. A few years later the baron was framed on homosexual charges by a neighbour with whom he was engaged in land disputes. The islanders turned against him, closed ranks, refused to help clear his name, although he had never violated any of the peasant boys. The baron was sent to prison where he died several years later of syphilis.

Apparently for years the baron's photographs circulated discreetly among homosexual aesthetes. In the early eighties someone donated a portfolio of his photos for an AIDS benefit and suddenly his work became famous. Today his photos fetch thousands of pounds a print, Ilia explained.

Ilia was a photographer. He was also a dealer and a collector. He had never seen the photos 'in the flesh', he explained. This is why he planned to take the midnight ferry and drive through the French countryside, arriving in Paris at dawn to catch the opening of the exhibition.

I didn't say a thing, but perhaps it showed in my face. We were sitting on the spindly metal chairs of the gallery café. I didn't say a thing, but when he described it I thought, that would be heaven: to be driving a car along the empty highways through the quiet countryside in the middle of the night. To arrive in Paris with the market-trading lorries and the muttering priests as the sun breaks over the city. To speed with a stranger through the dark, sleeping villages, making up lives, exchanging stories in the warmth of a fast car while the world recedes behind you.

When the waitress took away our tea he said, 'Come with me to Paris.'
I can't, I replied; I haven't got a nightgown.

He picked me up that evening. We didn't talk much on the drive to Dover; he was concentrating on the traffic. There were a lot of lorries at that time of night. His speedometer cut out at 200 k's; he usually drove at 195.

'You can be as correct and proper and rule-bound as you like,' he said, 'but the only way to guarantee survival is to anticipate the other guy.'

However fast he happened to be driving, he always sped up when he passed another car. 'You can never be sure what the other guy will do,' he explained. 'This is where you are your most vulnerable.' He couldn't bear to have anything in front of him: 'These guys, you don't know: they swerve, they brake, their wheels roll away. It is not good to have things in front of you.'

Ilia had been a spy, a political activist, a prisoner in labour camps and mental hospitals: 'Guns, knives, poisons, these things are for show and tell. If you want to kill a man the neatest way to do it is with a long pin in the ear.' He told me this at the top of the Eiffel Tower late one afternoon when the city was shrouded in yellow dusk and it looked like the end of the world.

At Dover there was a ferry waiting. As we stopped at customs Ilia handed my passport through the open window. When it was returned he zipped it into his pocket along with his own.

Can I have my passport please?

'Leave it with me. We'll have to show it on the other side.'

I'd rather carry it myself.

'What, you don't trust me?' Then he smiled. 'No, it's good; you don't trust nobody. It's a good thing.' Then he handed back my passport. 'But me, you can trust,' he added. 'You will see.'

The passage was rough because the boat was so empty. There were only three other cars and a couple of lorries in the hold. When we climbed up on the deck there were hardly any passengers or crew around. He led me through the ferry to the bar at the far end. There was nobody in the room, the bar was shut up tight with metal cages covering the bottles, but along the edges of the room were benches nailed against the wall. 'Sleep,' he said, taking my coat, patting the seat. I didn't like being ordered around but at that point I felt too rocky to resist. I lay down. He knelt on the floor beside me, patted my cheek, brushed back my hair. He was like a father, like a lover. 'Sleep,' he crooned. I closed my eyes. It felt better with my eyes closed. The bench swayed up and down beneath me. 'It's fucking the waves,' he murmured into my ear.

I woke at the announcement that we were arriving in Calais. Ilia was standing over me, watching me sleep. 'Don't hurry, there is plenty of time.'

We were the first ones off the boat. When the guard handed back our papers Ilia passed mine straight to me. I don't know where the other cars could have gone, but they didn't follow us through the village, out onto the highway. We didn't pass a single person, animal or car.

For hours we drove. 'Sleep,' he crooned. I wouldn't. Couldn't. I've always held this naive belief that as long as I'm awake nothing bad can happen. 'Sleep,' he repeated.

I want to see the dawn, I lied.

'I'll wake you when it comes.'

I'm not tired. I tried not to yawn. Shall I drive?

'Tomorrow,' he replied.'Tomorrow. When it's light. I'll drive us through the dark.'

We passed a few rabbits on the road, scurrying across the highway. Then suddenly he pulled into a petrol station. The petrol gauge read full but Ilia claimed it didn't work.

'Besides,' he grinned, 'we'll have to get you coffee if you're determined not to sleep.'

There were already two men at the bar, talking quietly. I didn't see their trucks outside but Ilia said he'd noticed them parked across the road. The man behind the counter nodded at Ilia and pulled out a shot glass. Ilia shook his head and called for two strong coffees. The other men looked up briefly then turned back to their conversation. They must have thought he was one of them. He looked like a trucker: he was small and smooth like a torpedo, he was coiled up like a spring, he wore a little woollen hat and a big jacket and he walked with a rolling gait, his hips moving from side to side, taking up much more space than one would think for a man his size.

He must have looked like a trucker and I must have looked like some hooker he had picked up. The thought amused me.

'Why do you smile?' he whispered, brushing his cheek against my ear. 'Tell me, what are you thinking?'

I think they think I'm a hooker.

'What is this, hooker?' he asked. He was Russian, Jewish, Czech: I never got it straight. He had lived in Oslo, Prague, Copenhagen, Cracow, Leningrad. He had lived all over Europe it seemed, but I never could quite pin down where he was born and what nationality he was. His passport was Swiss; 'I also have others,' he grinned. 'Norwegian, American, Hungarian . . .' But somehow in all those countries he'd never encountered the word before.

A hooker: a whore, a prostitute, a woman of the night, I explained.

'Oh this I know. But you are not a hooker,' he added solemnly.

A woman of easy virtue, I said.

'A what?'

An easy lay.

'I think you like adventure, yes? A bit of a gambler perhaps?'

Yes, I suppose. I don't know. I'm a coward really, you know, I protested; I've never done this before. Really.

He smiled. I wasn't sure whether he believed me. I didn't really care.

The door opened. A little man with thick glasses hurried in. It was black outside; until he opened the door I'd forgotten how black it was. It made the room inside seem spectacularly bright.

The man was carrying two huge sacks, like body bags. They were filled with bread. He scurried into the kitchen, then returned several minutes later with three metal baskets full of croissants which he spaced along the bar.

Ilia reached for a couple of croissants. They were still warm from the oven. He ordered two more coffees and dragged the sugar bowl towards him. His fingers were surprisingly long: artist's fingers. He reached into the bowl and pulled out a lump of sugar which he dipped quickly into his cup then sucked. 'A canard' we called it when I was a child. We'd sneak them from my grandmother's coffee tray while it waited outside the dining room after dinner.

Ilia dipped his sugarlump again and put it to my lips. It crumbled in my mouth. 'I'm sorry,' I said as the sugar dribbled down my chin.

'There is only one suck in each sugar,' he said. 'I meant for you to eat it.'

I don't like sugar, I explained.

'You'll need the energy.'

We left a few minutes later. As the car pulled away from the station I noticed two trucks parked across the road. You were right, I remarked; they must have belonged to the men at the counter.

'I am always right. No, not always,' he added. 'Usually.'

Driving at night. Dawn always seems to be breaking right behind you, leaving you driving into the dark. Lights suddenly emerge from the black. Sweep up behind, engulf you, transforming from some monstrous dinosaur into a shape, a form, a truck or car or motorbike. Then they disappear.

The sky. The clouds. Shapes emerge: black on black, roll and sway and crash and tumble into each other, disappear, returning to the indistinguishable wash. Then the tones: blueblack, greyblack, blue and grey. Then the sulphurous yellows. Then the pinks – suddenly the pinks: blood pinks, sinister pinks. Then somehow it becomes clean. Pink on white, blue on white, pink and blue: a baby's cradle.

Paris is between my thighs. Gauloises and Gitanes and the spikes of Montmartre and the Eiffel Tower. All the sulphur and the ash, the blueblack spires disappearing into the hungry pink mouth of the Seine at dawn.

The problem is you enter these things in a spirit of adventure. An experience. Nothing more. And you don't care about the other guy, so you let down all the barriers.

You expose everything: your greed, your desire, your fantasies – you show it all.

But then, of course, when the walls are down, people climb inside.

And after all that intimacy you can't help but be moved. And once you realize that you care about the other person, that you're interested – not in love, not even lust, simply simple interest – then you're hooked. You're trapped. Then the other person thinks, 'Yes,' thinks, 'yes, this person could make my life work.' And sometimes even you think, well fuck it, why not? Why not make his life work?

'You fuck like a tiger. Your body so strong, like an eel, like a wildcat, like a leather coil. You've opened the gate. You're taking me through . . .'

You think, yes, I could do it, I could climb into this person's life, I could make this man's life work. This is the first, the fatal mistake.

Ilia is the person with whom I explored perversions. Oh, we tried it all: handcuffs, leather, whips and rubber. Sometimes it was fascinating. Sometimes it was . . . well, eventually it all becomes just another game.

That first night, driving to Paris, we stopped once more, beside the river. Dawn was breaking. He needed a pee. He went down to the river. I crouched behind a rock. We walked along the bank a bit. I shivered; it was cold. He put his arm around me. He was warm, hot, his body was hot and hard as a brick. Then we got back into the car and proceeded to Paris.

It was dawn as we drove through the Porte de Clingancourt. 'You're tired.' I was. 'We'll find a place to stay.' Once we'd arrived I felt I could sleep. It would be OK. 'Do you know a hotel?' I realized then he was the type who usually slept in his car. There is a place on the Ile de la Cité that I try to get into each time I'm in Paris. Each time it is full. We drove to the Pont Neuf and parked. I found the hotel. In the square in front of it an old man dressed in blue was sweeping. One café was open. It must have stayed open all night. On the front door of the hotel was the sign: *complet*.

I pushed open the door. Ilia followed behind me. We walked up the two narrow flights to the *concierge*. She was sitting upright in a chair in the tiny room with all the keys behind her. Yes it was early. No they didn't have a room. No they wouldn't have one later, they were *complet*. Like the sign said on the front door. Yes she knew a place which might have something. She gave us directions, wrote down the name on the back of a card.

We found the hotel she recommended, it was on the corner where the rue de l'Ancienne Comédie meets four other streets. This was an ancient comedy: April in Paris, Ilia and me. There was a market nearby, the streets were slowly filling up with people. The café on the corner had a man outside reading his paper. A woman was walking a dog, a black and white spotted dog, a Dalmatian. A man in a grey suit strode by with an umbrella. We pushed open the door and walked again up two steep flights to a small room. A young woman nodded, irritated. Yes they had a room, yes it was empty now, yes it was free for one or two nights. But it was a triple. They had no doubles, no singles. I looked at Ilia: 'We'll take it,' he said.

'Don't you want to see it first?'

'We'll take it, whatever it is.'

We paid for two days in advance. She gave us the key and directed us up three more flights to the top of the building.

The room was oval-shaped with a curve, like a shrine, in one corner. It had three small beds jammed in together, a hook on the wall and nothing else. The radiator dripped a green trickle of liquid onto the damp, brown carpet. At the end of the room a full-length window with a lace curtain and an iron balcony looked over the corner where the five streets intersected.

It was a perfect room, a beautiful room, a perfect room for the situation. The beds were like medieval racks, the springs stuck up like spikes through the flimsy mattress, they creaked when you walked past them on the floor, they were covered in greying linen and a single orange blanket. Each one was more uncomfortable than its neighbour. I dumped my bags on the nearest bed.

I'll take this one, I said, curling up to sleep.

'Can I come in with you?' he said.

There didn't seem to be much point in refusing.

We fucked for several hours, then I fell asleep.

That night we were walking round the city; it was after midnight. We'd bought a crêpe from one of those little corner holes where Arab men sit like penitents across a dimly-lit counter, behind a barrier of canned drinks and blackboards listing twenty-seven different fillings, each of which comes from a dented tin. I later discovered that Ilia didn't like restaurants. He was prepared to sit in an outdoor café for a short coffee and brandy, for the time it takes to skim the personal ads in the *Herald Trib*. Then he'd pop up saying he was bored or cold or hot and disappear in search, he said, of a loo; though I saw him, each time he disappeared, plugging coins into the pay phone beside the urinal.

One afternoon I dragged him into a restaurant. He walked to the farthest corner and sat with his back to the wall. But I want to watch the people, I complained; you're just going to read your paper anyway. He read the *Herald Tribune* every day. And at least one other newspaper. *The New York Times*, some German paper, sometimes *Le Monde*.

But he was adamant: 'If you insist on coming to a restaurant I will sit where I choose.' So I spent the meal watching Ilia rustling his papers.

It is comforting to find that even the most bizarre encounters soon become domestic.

After that I sat in outdoor cafés or ate shish-kebabs or hot-dogs or one of the other varieties of carrion comfort sold on the streets.

That first night we were wandering around the flower market on the Ile St Louis. I was teasing Ilia, hiding behind benches, popping out from the edges of buildings.

'I will have to tie you down,' he said.

Try it! I teased and darted down a corridor between a row of locked greenhouses.

As we wandered across the Seine and he told me about Chartres, the secret societies of masons who built the medieval cathedrals. And Monteverdi's *Vespers* which he contrasted with the requiem form. The heaviness of the agnostic Mozart, the lightness of the atheist Fauré. How do you know all these things? I asked as we walked along the tow path.

The lights of passing barges bore down on us like trains. A barrage, an assault of music and laughter and loudspeakers describing the scene to the drunken celebrants. The blinding lights obliterated Paris as they passed, shimmering in the water like a glass moon shattered. Then the lights and the noise would recede leaving a greater, darker silence in their wake. And we walked on a few minutes further till the next *bateau ivre* descended.

How do you know all these things? I whispered as his hand explored my thigh against the inner arches of the Pont Notre-Dame.

'I know everything,' he said. 'I know everything about you. All your fantasies and fears,' he said. 'I am you,' he whispered.

It was a silly line but I wanted to believe him; it sent a shiver down my spine.

Later, when we made our way back to the hotel where the five streets converged, it was just beginning to get light. From the Arab in his little niche we bought a bottle of cheap champagne. I was exhausted, ready to crash. The *concierge* looked up from her TV. She nodded as we passed, then turned back to her black and white romance or horror.

In the room I flopped on the nearest bed. I was recounting a story of my childhood. About a dog I had, a spotted dog, black and white. It was run over by a car one summer when I was away; the first summer I was away from home, on my own, staying with friends of friends who lived in Paris. My first trip abroad. My first time in Paris. A cultural exchange. And the dog who was my only companion in the world. Killed. I chattered on, looking at the ceiling, laughing a little at the melodrama of the tale.

Ilia was getting undressed around me. I heard the zipper of his case opening and closing, the bang of his belt against the floor. He was murmuring moues of sympathy, chuckling when a response was required. Suddenly he was standing above me, a snap and my hand was encased in metal, pinching the skin of my wrist.

I stared at it a moment.
An endless moment.
Trying to form the thought.

Then I struggled.

He was on top of me, his whole body pinning mine to the bed. My other wrist was trapped in his grip.

'Don't struggle,' he said very quietly. I could see the whites of his eyes, the smooth shine of his forehead in the lights from the streetlamp outside. We'd kept the light off at my request: I hate the glare of overhead light, especially from an uncovered bulb.

'Don't struggle,' he said, his voice a stony monotone. 'I'm stronger than you, you'll only get hurt.'
I struggled on for maybe one spasm, maybe several minutes or hours. Everything coalesced in that struggle.

One is always – almost always – watching the drama. But in these first few seconds or minutes or hours I was no longer the spectator. I was the terrorist, the murderer, the battered woman, the abused child. Engaged. I was engaged. Then the other selves returned.

I knew he was right. Still I struggled – a little? A lot? Then I conceded.

He snapped the other hand in. A moment of stillness. Suspension. His eyes watching me watching him looking for a clue.
Then it passed.

He shrugged, grinned: 'You were really scared.'

I was.

'But you asked for it, you told me to do this.'

What!

'When you were hiding in the dead flowers I said I'd have to chain you down. And you said, you said, and your eyes gleamed thick and red and you said . . .'

. . . Just try it.

This is the problem with foreigners. Words mean what they say. You can't hide behind them, words don't mean what they mean, they mean what they say. Humpty Dumpty said when I use a word it means what I choose it to mean. Alice was too puzzled to reply. When it's your own language you forget what the words really say anymore.

No, I meant, I said, lying in the unlit room as dawn broke over Paris and a stranger like a mallet towered naked pinning my arms to the bed. No, what I meant was . . .

It wasn't worth explaining. The moment had passed and already we were mired in the swamp again. Already he was pulling a tiny key from his pocket. Wait a minute, I said. I'd noticed the tiny key earlier, dangling from the chain in the ignition of the car; I'd assumed it belonged to some small locked box. Now that we're here we might as well . . . I mean . . . I struggled as he tried to unlock the right hand.

'No, you didn't want it. I misunderstood.'

You're right, I didn't, I explained, protecting my chains, pulling my cuffed hand from his key. But now that we've gone this far let's see what you were proposing to do.

'To do? I don't know,' he sulked, wrenching my hand, forcing the key into the lock. 'This isn't a play, you know, it isn't all scripted. I didn't know what I was going to do.'

Let's just improvise, I suggested, sitting up, rubbing my wrist where the metal had bitten it. He threw me the key and slunk into the corner of the room.

'I don't know what it means, this word, this "improvise".'

I explained.

'No,' he muttered.

Please.

'No,' he replied with a little more force, but the gleam returned to his eye.

The next morning he went off to his exhibition and returned that afternoon with a whip. For an instant the high returned, the moment where everything freezes and you're caught in the tantalizing question of what happens next.

I locked him to the bed. I stroked his thighs, his buttocks. And then and then . . .

It's the anticipation much more than the actual pain. It's the illusion of power . . . never more than an illusion unless you intend to take it to the end – because you always know that you will be there next time, under the whip, the cuff, the cloak, under the leather, the metal, the rubber . . .

If you play your games at night it's all right. You lie back, exhausted, and sleep and wake into daylight. Life goes on.

If you play your games in daylight there's the slow climbing down from the illusion, from the fantasy of power, which always leaves you lower than the place where you began.

The problem with Ilia was he understood that it was a game. By the time I realized this, I had played too long. I fell for the illusion so I blamed him for being real.

When I was a child I knew that Santa Claus and the Tooth Fairy and Adam and Eve were all fairytales, but somehow I always believed in leprechauns. When my mother went to Ireland I made her promise to bring me one. I carefully drilled her in the rules and etiquette of leprechauns. She promised that she wouldn't take her eyes off him, night or day. And so I waited, fantasizing about my constant magical companion. My first instructions to him would be: never disappear, never go away and leave me.

When my mother returned with a little wooden leprechaun I threw a tantrum, I screamed until I was sick and refused to even hold the doll. I wouldn't speak to my mother for weeks. She thought I understood. She thought we were playing a game of leprechauns. Even now, as I tell the story, I can't quite forgive her for failing to secure a real one for me.

And so Ilia had to go.

I packed up the whips and the straps and the odd little books and the exotic devices, the clips and ticklers and bracelets, and balls, the bibelot of centuries of erotics from places like Jakarta and Bangkok. While the west was wallowing in wattle and daub, worshipping monolithic stones, the orientals were writing the *Kamasutra* (Sanskrit: Kama, love; Sutra, science), refining perversions to perfection.
Ilia was a scientist.

What remains? The mystery. The fantasies. Why did Ilia read the *Herald Tribune* twice a day? These are the things I recall late at night, not the lick of the lash or the flicker of anticipation when every nerve is waiting for the pain to lay its salty kiss. It's the odd phrase which strikes . . . The most efficient way to kill a man . . . The classic profile of a terrorist . . . Oh, don't worry about speeding, the cops will look up my number on their computer and then wave me on.

We never were stopped for speeding; not in England, France or Germany, not in Italy or Spain. We sped at 200 k's night and day, from Barcelona to Le Havre, and never once were we picked up for speeding. So I'll never know if what he said was true.

19 Delay Due to Body

The trains are slow today. The train/tube/subway/metro/underground.
Delay due to body . . . Due to staff shortages. To investigations.
By order of the Police/Secret Service/Fire Brigade. Trains will be non-stopping . . .

Press to call lift. Automatic service. There will be no lift. Restricted headroom . . . Way out. Way in.

Stockwell via Bank via Charing Cross via . . .

The man sitting beside you is staring at your reflection in the window across the aisle.

The train empties slowly. Three, two, one person left.

The man sits beside you. All the other seats are empty. It is you and him in this too-bright lighted carriage in the long, dark tunnel, rattling at speed. Not fast enough. He's watching your reflection and you're staring at your feet or the door or the ceiling. The knobs swing obscenely, like balls on a tupping ram: safety straps – no safety in them. You can't break away; you can't simply stand up and walk off, move down to the far end of the carriage, because that would be admitting . . .

Fear inspires the bully. Is this a challenge? Is this how it happens? Is this the moment . . .? The minutes between stations when anything can happen? The hours between night and day, three to six am when the light flows back and everything slows down again and fear ebbs away; these are the hours when most rapes take place.

The man beside you is staring at your reflection in the window across the aisle. You refuse to engage with him.

You refuse to look. The knobs are madly tossing back and forth, rocking near and far, attached by their thick springs to the safety bar above. The man turns his head. He looks at you directly now. He's looking right at you. His nose to your ear. Your eyes to the floor.

The train thumps and rattles, the noise fills the spaces, disguising your breathing, his words: he is speaking. He is whispering something. You can't hear the words. Drowned in the scream of the train through the tunnel. It's slowing, it shivers. It shudders to a halt.

The carriage door opens. Two people enter. The man beside you gets up and walks away.

When I was a child we lived at the top of a hill overlooking the river. In winter the hill became an ice mountain, perfect for tobogganing, although we were forbidden. If you shot across the lawn at the bottom into the river, if you fell through the ice, you were finished. The current. Even strong swimmers, even if the cold didn't numb them, the current would certainly carry them off.

Under the ice. The smothering blanket, the brittle, impenetrable ceiling of ice. Under the sheltering sky of ice. The pull of the river under the ice was a current that nobody could resist.

Of course we did it anyway, we shot down the mountain when no one was watching.

Some winters the ice was pinched and mottled, like a diseased skin. Some winters it was black and luscent like liquid ebony. If you put your face right down to it you could see little bits: twigs, debris, perhaps even fishes, even frogs and tadpoles, water snakes trapped, fossilized in the dark wall of ice which plunged right into the heart of the river.

Some winters it was clear, almost white, almost porcelain. Those were the seasons you could see the cracks: crisscrossing the wall's face, vertical, horizontal, cracks like the veins in a huge slab of marble. Those were the seasons we hesitated longest before plunging, inevitably once again, to the frosty flight.

One year a child got too hot with the exertions of climbing back, dragging the squeaking wooden toboggan behind her all the way back up the hill. She took off her jacket and lay on the ice to cool off.

What I remember is the steam. No dry dead frost of words in the cold; it was moist this steam, it was hot, alive. It made us laugh. We all gathered round to watch the steam rise, the steam where her body kissed the ice.

Next time I saw her was in the coffin, wrapped in the same icy blanket of white. Pneumonia. We all had to gather to sing hymns as the mouth sucked her into its fiery maw.

She was too hot before, now she was burning.

In Barcelonetta late one night after eating fish on the beach, under a full moon, the serenading waves, the Gypsy Kings blasting from every juke box, we stumbled into a bar, M and I, or was it R then? Or perhaps it was Joe? I have introduced Joe before. No, it couldn't have been him, he was the richest man I knew; he never could afford to move beyond the circuit of the race track.

Barcelonetta. It was too late for a taxi and all the tubes back to the city had shut. There was only one light left in the village. It belonged to a bar, a tiny bar jammed in a street of high-rises, packed out with people. Two faded women – hookers – stood outside drinking. Some unwritten rule – or perhaps it was written, I never mastered the Catalonian – by some authority the women remained on the street while the men kept them supplied with drink. Men. Boys. The place swarmed with drugged-up teenagers and one old man. The man poured a whisky for R then he pulled out a coke for me – didn't ask, just assumed that I would drink coke. Then he drew R aside and whispered: I'm your man.

Anything you want, you ask me. Anything.

We mused on that for several days.

On the wall at the back of the bar, perched on the top of the juke box, was a tiny metropolis of birdcages. Piled side by side and on top of each other, a sky-scraping forest of birdcages. Each cage had a large bird inside it. The cages were vibrating from the pulse of a juke box below them.

Like clockwork each of the birds was pecking the ceiling of its own cage. Demented. A forest of caged birds darting in time to the music. Like some embryonic creature stabbing away at the engulfing egg, like some child, trapped, drowning under the curved umbrella of ice. Pecking to death to the beat of the Gypsy Kings. Like some nightmarish wind-up mechanical toy . . .

Anything you want, you ask me. Anything.

20 Food and Comfort

What bothered me, what really upset me was that there was nothing to say.

Hi. Hello. How are you fine and you fine well bye. Then he drifts rather vaguely, embarrassed, off.

This person who knew you so intimately, who explored all your fantasies. I knew nothing of his life. I couldn't ask: how's your girlfriend/daughter/wife? I only knew he had a woman because I'd seen her through the window one night when I begged for an emergency session. I couldn't even ask, how's your garden? since his consulting room faced the road. I only knew he had a garden because I'd sneaked a peek through the fence one August break when he was away.

This hunger to know another person.

All the lives going on without you. Walking by the river at dusk when the lights are on in the houses lining the embankment before the curtains are closed against passing, prying eyes. Families sitting in their gardens, sitting round their suppers, sitting together in front of the TV. The single woman peering in; the voyeur. There's no place for you, my love. Pretending not to notice, not to mind that there's no place for you at the table.

'Oh, it's a sad business,' Anna mutters, reaching to retrieve the cigarette from my lips.

What, therapy?

'No, life.'

She was the sort who preferred white food. Fish, not flesh, not shellfish that had to be prized from its shell: cod and sole, nothing pink or robust like a salmon. Anorexic I imagine, though she never mentioned it. She like jellies, yoghurts, anaemic vegetables: courgettes and mushrooms. Salads she'd drown in vinegar, wilting the lettuce, obscuring any subtlety of leaf or herb. Every morning she would squeeze herself a large glass of lemon juice to mortify the flesh.

White wine. Clear perfume. Martini, gin, vodka; drinks with no colour. Peaches and pears, apples and apricots, anything that was almost white when you peeled it – she couldn't stomach the skins.

The first time we met was an initiation session for the foreign students in the residence. The dining room was the only place we really had to be. Once a day. Checked in, checked out. The other twenty-three hours we were left to ourselves. To grow up. To blow up. To stick our fingers down our throats and throw it all up.

She would appear at the evening meal, on her cheek a tear-shaped scrape, from falling on rocks, she'd say. Charming, cheerful, she chattered with the others, eager to be helpful: cleared the plates, washed the cups, hovered on the edges, smoking cigarettes, or after dark sucking her thumb.
Desperate to belong. Desperate. Terrified.

Seventeen; her hands cross-hatched with scratches. She picked her scab when no one looked; it wept two great teardrops of blood which ran down her cheek, staining her shirt or the sofa where she sat so no one would ever forget that she had been there, though nobody would ever quite remember who she was.

Temptations. The pearls in the shop window, the man in the street, the ice-cream, cream cake, cakes and ale. Naughty but nice. Consuming. Being consumed. I was at this party. It was too full of people. And food. I couldn't stop. Looking around it seemed that everybody else was eating too. More slowly perhaps than I was, or smaller bites, but they were all eating.

I was chewing on some thick, greasy thing. Already I was feeling sick, but I just kept on at it, chewing away. Pushing my way to the buffet, to the plate, to the piece after piece of this stuff, that stuff, anything just consume a whale dies if it ever stops eating is it a whale no maybe it's a shark something sinister that doesn't sing.

(I once read of a bulimic who used to binge then puke then eat her own vomit.)

Finally I decided the only way to quit consuming all this shit was to leave.

The voices, the laughter, the bubbles of conversation, rising, tinkling like champagne in a glass. The shuddering silence as you close the door behind you. Alone on the landing.
Listening to your footsteps echo down the hall, you wonder: am I sober?

Opening the front door to the rush of cold air: what if I get picked up for being over the limit?

I scrape back my hair, stick on a tape of Glenn Gould performing the *Goldberg Variations*. Nobody could stop a woman in a prim ponytail listening to piano. So I risk it.

The notes dart from the machine, rising to the roof of the car, pecking at the ceiling, desperate but nonetheless demure, never losing their composure in their efforts to escape from the confines of the manuscript, the musician's fingers, the ivory keys, the plastic tape, the metal box, the little rusty car slipping slowly through London/Paris/Madrid, turning too smoothly, stopping too gently, every movement calculated not to draw attention to the performer, the performance.

Eventually, when I am almost home and can't stand it any longer – this pecking of the notes against my ceiling – I unroll the window and release them.

Abandoned. Free-falling into the anonymous night.

Pulling down the tins, packets of old biscuits, cakes, pasta, reading the small print: best before: June '82, December '86, January '84 . . . Another hungry night.

You must learn to take care of yourself. You must feed yourself properly. Nobody else is going to do it.

Back again in the bookshop. Surely I deserve better . . . ? My time is worth . . .

To whom? Says who?

I always expected . . .

You have to accept that you are what you are.

And what about that thesis I was writing? I was writing, I was writing, I think, about . . . Picasso.

Excuse me, miss, do you have that new book? The one that tells you what to do with stuff that is left over, that's on the turn, that's going off.

Fishing with the customers, staring at them, flashing a smile, catching this eye, that lip, hooking this or that man, like hitching: I can make you look at me. Pick me up: *'Tiramisu.'* Take me away from this place, kind sir. The bodies. The casualties.

My woman friends say that I'm beautiful, my men never say more than I'm attractive, sometimes striking, occasionally interesting: the ominous 'interesting', like 'nice' – you have nice hands.

Nice: what does it mean? Vanilla, an absence of colour, of flavour. 'You look interesting, your looks are interesting, you have interesting looks.'

Perhaps you don't reveal your beauty to men.
Perhaps they simply haven't the eyes to see it.

This one looks a good bet: a father – you can tell by the washable T-shirt, the fluorescent plastic watch, the bags under his eyes.

That one looks rich: look at the shoes. He takes good care – or his wife does.

I think I'd like an architect, someone who knows how to build things. Someone who knows how things fit together. How things work.

I long for an uncomplicated transaction; a simple exchange of affection.

No, be honest, be bold: what I long for is simply love.

Not the subtleties and subtexts, the constructs and deconstruction, the analyzing and interpreting and replaying over and over again. I long for that vegetable love. I want to be that carved stone Madonna warming her face in the sun.

Dear Mum: it is the marmalade season: *Marie est malade.*

Some mornings I wake up and I long to shout, No! Wait! There's been some awful mistake! It wasn't meant to be like this. I was supposed to be a mother by now: children, a husband, a garden, a pretty terraced house, a car, a dog, a cottage in the country. What's gone wrong? Somebody please do something, make it right, it isn't my fault. And time is running out.

Darling, you'd be bored rigid, you'd run a mile faced with screaming babies and the prospect of three squares on the table with the in-laws every second Sunday.

What I remember is the smell in the back of the cupboards. The smell of cumin ('come in').

The flat was empty. The previous tenants left a wastepaper basket full of rubbish – the odd bits in the backs of drawers: buttons, pins, elastic bands curling like worms in the corners of rooms, under the carpet. But the carpet was lifted and removed, like a stone the worm lives under, and the worm remains, oblivious, when the stone is rolled away.

The kitchen was surprisingly clean. White, formica cupboards. Someone had actually tried to clean them. In the light from the window you could see the swirls where the cloth had been: swirls of dirt, like a child's finger-painting.

I opened the door and there it was. Suddenly. It swept into the room. The warm, sweet smell. The spicy smell. The comforting smell of cold winter evenings and being safe, inside, in front of the fire.

Cumin. The delicate hint. The smell of chilli on a Sunday night. Birthday food. Celebration. She always begged for hotter food, hotter and hotter. Self-immolation: burning from the inside out. Sometimes on the cold winter nights it feels like you'll never be warm again.

How much cumin can one consume in a lifetime? All the plastic bags of spices straining at the edges like a pregnant woman's belly.

Somewhere it sits, on some dusty shelf. The brown-red, blood-red, rusty-red slowly fading with the scent, the smell, the spice drying out in some cupboard in some long abandoned house.

The cupboards in the flat were bare. It was only the smell that remained. Not even a telltale rim of red where the jar had stood.

Cumin, piled in carmine mounds in market places in Barcelona, in Istanbul, in Rio de Janeiro.

Rue, myrrh and cumin to clear the sphynx's rheumy eyes.

Moving, moving, always moving, always starting somewhere new. Alone again. And all the other people's lives hum busily about you. People in couples, people in pairs, nobody walks on these streets alone . . .

21 Truth Dare Consequences

Licking the fencepost. Iron spikes, black against the blanketing snow. You know your tongue will stick, its heat like a solder welding your flesh with the metal. Still you do it. You were dared to; you have no choice; you do.

And they all disappear, giggling, as the night descends, the darkness. And you, stuck by your bleeding tongue to this spike on the cage, keeping the wild dogs at bay. Are they behind you or approaching . . . ?

You can't turn, your eyes only ease to the edges of your head, seeking the slight . . . the silent . . . the whisper of paws racing over ice. The snap of a leaf as the wild dogs leap.

Till your tears and time and twisting finally tear your lacerated tongue from its stake.

Dare; you dared; you did it. You won. You met the challenge. You didn't retreat. So what?

What can you say about a small town? Truth was never possible; too many versions circulated.

No place is ever big enough: the County, the Province, the Country, the Continent, the Hemisphere, the World, the Galaxy, the Universe. My Very Early Marriage Suited Uncle Neptune Just Perfectly. Or was it Just Suited? Which comes first, Pluto or Saturn?

By these simple words we locate ourselves. A body from Pluto or Venus could identify a single person from all the billions of billions of the earth's population by these few hieroglyphs.

But what of the beggar woman on the streets of Bangladesh with no address to name her?

Consequences. Nobody knows the consequences. Some people never suffer them. Some people live with them all their lives. Truth, Dare, Consequences. The sins of the father . . .

Promise or Repeat. Repeat.
Repeat was a cheat, but most of us took it.
But you could only do it once. Repeat.

Word games played behind the Co-op: weekday evenings sitting on the dusty grain sacks, smoking stolen cigarettes. When the boys arrived we'd drag the sacks, like concrete, their shapes slowly shifting if two or three grabbed a corner and heaved, adjusting to the tension, elongating with the effort. But not even the boys could convince us there were bodies inside. The sacks were too dense, too solid; we could barely even dent them.

Every summer evening we built the sacks into fortresses: towers of Babel at the back of the Co-op where the farm trucks came to load in the morning.

The white gritty gravel. The chalky pigeon-shit. The sour smell of grain fermenting. And always there was a body; a swallow's corpse, battered in the sudden sluice of grain from the chute; a mouse, dry and crushed like some little furry spot in the road. Darren McKinnis threw it at me once: a dead mouse. I thought it was some autumn flower dried soft in the heat of the harvest fields.

Darren McKinnis. I hated him even then, even though I prayed he would kiss me. 'Necking', I believe is the term. He was the only one left. Even he had higher standards than to neck with me. The sad thing is, I still respect him for it.

Ten, twelve, fourteen; sweet sixteen. I'll have to hire a gigolo or be raped, I moaned to my best friend; the hole will close up tight and then I'll never have a baby.

We piled the sacks, one on top of the other; you had to jump from the very top, launching off its slippery edge in the fading evening light onto the gravel gleaming below. Inevitably the girls gave out first. They were bored; it was boring. And they understood the rules.

As the only girl who had never been kissed I felt obliged to stick it out after the others had gone home. Me and Darren McKinnis dragging the sacks back into place. If we left them out the Co-op would know we'd been there. It would be my fault, mine and his, if the Co-op ever found out and forbade us all to play there.

When he grew up he became a psychiatric nurse. Heaving bodies, bland as grain sacks.

Drinking champagne; it goes down the wrong way. Drowning in champagne. Struggling for air. Surfacing in the swimming pool. Six years old, surfacing from your second belly-flop off the high diving board.

This is the way to do it: cling and cling to the outer edge of the high diving board as the queue backs up behind you.

'Give up,' people cry from the pool-side below.
'Come down; it's all right.'
'Don't be scared, don't be ashamed.'

People before you have done it, people much older than you; they have inched their way back along the board, sliding, toe to heel, to the safety of the handrail. Then, step by backwards step, they make their way down the ladder to the chlorine-smelling puddles round the base of the high diving board.

You could do it. You could just retreat.

But suddenly that moment when the humiliation of defeat overcomes the knowledge of sure death . . .

You drop, falling from the top of the high diving board to belly-flop into the gleaming, grinning, teasing, taunting polka-dot blue of the pool below.

Again and again and again that summer.

I never did learn to dive.

The following year I avoided swimming pools altogether.

This is not the way to proceed.

I've always preferred oceans anyway. They terrify me; the relentless waves enveloping . . .

And there's no way back.
And there's no way to say no.

Does this suggest interference? Child abuse is the fashion these days. We were all abused in one way or another. Is violation simply in the mind? Some people are born victims. And the violator always forgets. So who is ultimately to blame?

And what of the person who reads the symptomologies and suddenly experiences the symptoms – the sexual hypochondriac, the psychosomatic sexual victim? Is his/her pain any less than the person with bruises and a court order to show?

Then there's sad-eyed Lisa with her famous toothless grin. Lisa came from the farms behind the stone quarry. Barren land.

One summer she stopped coming to school. Nine months later she was sighted at the shopping centre with a tiny baby wrapped in a scrap of orange blanket.

Who would sleep with Lisa? Nobody would sleep with Lisa. Someone must have done it though. But winter came and she withdrew, back to the tyreless caravan that she shared with her father and myriad brothers. The next year it was all over.

True Crime: Summer Special: Skeleton in Lovers' Lane.

The reporters came, the social workers, child psychologists, psychiatrists conducting seminars and private sessions in the school gym. The town was famous for a week. Lisa's oldest brother was charged with the murder. They never worked out which one was responsible for the kid.

We were forbidden from the orchard known as Lovers' Lane that year. Lisa went to live in a home. And the dead baby? Well, it was one less burden on the state, somebody said.

When I was a child I met the Prime Minister. Late at night. My name had been drawn from the hat at school. Several teachers pointed out that I could pass the honour up if I chose; there was no obligation and a stream of students with better clothes (without the hair-lip, the cross-eye, the limp) would be happy to fight for the honour.
I held firm.

What I remember is the lights and the large polka-dotted bosom of the woman. She must have been his wife; the man himself I don't recall at all. In one chubby hand she clutched a handbag; a lace handkerchief seeped out the edges of her other fat fist.

When I passed her the bouquet she had to shift the handbag into the handkerchief hand, then pass the bouquet into the same hand to reach down and pat my head. So many hands: an octopus. I was terrified that she would not have enough and it would be my fault.

Somehow she managed. I curtseyed and the cameras flashed and I was taken home to bed.

'It's all right, darling, it wasn't your fault.'

22 Essential Questions

1. What do people do on weekends? How do people live? How do they survive when there is no work to go to?

2. Do you work? That's the essential question. Do you work? Meaning: what do you do? Meaning: who are you? What worth, what value, where do you rank?

Do you work? Of course I work, what else is there? Work, eat, sleep. Sex if you're lucky: *La Ronde*.

No, I mean do you have a job?

The other essential question: is he married?

Is he single? straight? solvent? reasonably sophisticated? No, scratch the last question; beggars can't be choosers. And if he is, why is he available? That's what I want to know; what's the matter with him that no one's snapped him up by now?

Finally the inevitable, unavoidable, no-longer-put-offable visit home to meet the mother. At least the father decamped decades ago. Women I can deal with. And what a relief not to have to flirt with some fat-fingered, nicotine-stained, whisky-breathed old lecher.

Who do you know? Where do you come from? All the conversations: stocks and bonds, clothes shops, jewellery.

Oh yes, I was in Ottawa once, cruising on the St Lawrence River; we pulled in at dawn.

I don't believe Ottawa is on the St Lawrence.

But of course it is; we arrived there at dawn.
Shall we resort to the atlas? Discretion is the better part . . . Besides she's a senile old lady. Senile as a snake in the sun.
Darling, but your new lady friend is so . . . forceful. Is she a socialist too?

You travel to a grey, raining city. The peacocks scream in the garden, the roses, glimpsed from the kitchen window, blowzy in the wind. This territory is familiar: the kitchen's too tiny, dishes greasy from poor washing, the food has a faint odour of mould, the hostess being too old to taste anyway. The biscuits are soft, the peanuts smell of cupboard, the cheese is leather, sweating grease.

In the rest of the house the elegant rooms harbour a few decent pieces: the walnut sideboard, the mahogany chest, the Chippendale dining chairs covered in psychedelic cotton, now faded to a uniform brown to blend with the carpet, the floor, the walls. The Limoges mixes with gas-station give-aways. Still, she notes the way you set the table: the napkin ring – do you take the biggest or the most discreet? The price of meat these days! Would you pick up a package of mushrooms, darling? A newspaper – oh no, don't bother, Celia next door passes hers on to me once a week. Now that's two pence I owe you for the pins. Don't bother, but of course I insist, dear, I can't have you going home saying his aged mother cheated you of two pence. And that's a pound you owe me from church this morning.

Dear Mum: the conversation meandered round to McNaught of McNaught. As soon as genealogy begins I tune out, but I did recall McNaught of McNaught: is he the good guy or the bad one? Should I have admitted to him?
When in doubt, play dumb.
I often find myself playing dumb these days.

Stumbling up the stony path to the 'Lady's Entrance' round the back. I attempt a joke as we titivate before the mirror: several generations and a rainbow of grey stands between us.

'Twenty years ago, dear, there was only one entrance; ladies were allowed in the bar in those days, we didn't have our own sitting room; it's much nicer now, don't you think?'

The men come in once an hour sporting an infinitesimal sherry to the three or four pints they've quaffed with the boys.

'Oh yes, much nicer without the men.'

And after the meal of English Empire we walk it off in the North Sea wind while she sleeps, secure in the Ladies' Lounge.

'She's so light, darling, your lady friend, you'd better hold her tight in this weather.'

'She' was the cat's mother, your mother used to say.

She sits in the room beside you, watching.

'Better tie a ribbon to her ankle in case she decides to float away.'

At lunch: Katherine, will you pass the mustard. Is he teasing? Is this a conspiracy to toughen up the name? Katherine, his mother echoes: now where was it that you studied? Ah, Oxford. What college? I'm not familiar with that one, is it one of the newer colleges? He dislikes names ending with 'ie', thinks they sound undignified. My namesake, I explain, smiling sweetly, threw herself out of a thirteenth-floor window into the traffic below. I'm attempting to distance myself from her; I'd prefer it if you call me by the name I use myself.

He looks at me, stroking his beard: angry? amused? Don't complain, don't explain. It's one of his mottoes; unlike so many of us who claim mottoes, he actually lives by his.

Later, waiting on the front steps for her to retrieve her umbrella, a uniformed man with a face like a raw steak: 'I'm sorry, madam, that's the Men's Entrance . . .'
Is it the absence of a penis or the fact of my womb which offends? I enquire. Sadly, she returns before he can muster a reply.

And driving home they point out the Manor House, the Terraced House in the Royal Crescent, the Georgian Town House, still impressive but nothing is quite what it was is it dear. And now even this is being eroded: the basement flat, then the attic rooms, and soon the prospect of paying guests 'pg's' invading the body of the place.

The elephant-foot umbrella stand from some old colonial uncle sits forlorn, rejected, its ridiculous, improbable toenails shining in the gloom.

Yes, in this five-storey house we move from room to room turning off the solitary, naked bulb as we go. The Chippendale now chipped beyond repair, but still supporting enough silver for the grandchildren from the New World to marvel: this is where we come from, this is what we were. Their flat vowels still oppress the smiling grandmother: this is what we have descended to.

The pennies. The daffs growing brown in their vases. The *familles rose* and *verte* intermingle with Tesco's and M&S.
Now who did you say your grandmother was?
Now was that family from Ireland or from London, my dear?

How does she live? What does she live on? What is she doing these days? Is she working? Meaning: does she have a job? A lover? A secret legacy?

She's living out her fantasies in a tiny row house on the edge of the city. No, she isn't working. No, she doesn't seem to be looking for a job.

Who knows what she's secretly selling off: family silver, pictures, twenties dresses all satin and cashmere and crepe de Chine, all fading into the softness of a spider's web, the sling, the hammock that protects her from the world. The fluff and buttons at the back of the drawer, the corner of the cabinet.

What does one do at the end of a line which began eight/ten generations ago? Younger sons from England, hot-heads, black sheep, n'er do wells. The dreamers and the doers, the remittance men and preachers making off with their measly promise of a New World, a savage landscape to be tamed.

They sailed up the St Lawrence with their accents and their history, stopping at Halifax and Montreal, at Ottawa and Toronto, Winnipeg, Saskatoon, Vancouver: all the British generals and French aristocrats and anonymous Indians leaving their names on the maps of this country.

Trappers and traders, woodcutters, lumberjacks, felling the trees, trapping the animals: maple, elm, birch, beech, jack pine, Douglas fir; wolf, beaver, bear, mink, otter, coon, rabbit, fox, seal, ermine, wolverine. Rivers of sap, rivers of blood flowing into the ocean to feed the insatiable motherland.

The families grew like cities: multiplied, divided. Then the train came, that artery, that river to the heartland, its two black lines taptapping to the farthest edge, from the sea to sea, two solitudes, 2,000 miles of frozen wasteland. Miles and miles of miles and miles. These distances; they terrify.

And in this neon century the fortunes receded. Where do they go?

She makes the backward journey, down the St Lawrence, up the Thames.

What does she live on? Walking through Wimbledon, wearing her grandmother's pearls like a talisman, seeking the house she knew in the bedtime stories, discovering that it no longer exists. The house was burned down in the war, leaving its name to a street, a park, a pub on the corner. The Pakistani newsagent's used to be a butcher's. Where the betting shop is was a chemist. The used car lot was a green grocer's.

Suddenly the words make sense: 'tomato' with a short 'a', 'flat', 'lift', 'petrol'.

'The butcher's on the corner. We would stop there every morning on the way to the park for Nanny to pick up the bones for her Billy. We all hated Billy, he scratched and chased cats and smelled like an old lady, but he gave us the excuse for a walk.' My grandmother, barely a whisper now. 'And every morning a great poet in his big, black cloak would swoop down on little Louisa in her pram and kiss and tickle her. Nanny would blush and we all tried to tempt him, but he only had eyes for the baby.'

'And who was this great poet, Gran?'

'Somebody Swinburne. I've never read his work; they say it isn't seemly. But he loved our Louisa.'

These claims to greatness: 'The day the Queen Mother was married. The congregation bowed like a wind blowing over a field of wheat when the new Queen swept past in her wedding gown with a double row of baby pages wafting her lacy train through the abbey.'

These are the things that she lives on: the blue plaques, the tow paths, the punts on the river, the kites on the Heath. They're changing the guard at Buckingham Palace. Yes, there is an England, she thinks as the black cab rushes the crossing, as the red double-decker lumbers past splashing oily mud on her blue stockings.

23 The Main

The Main is what separates east from west. It runs north and south from the river, straight through the city, miles and miles out to a place called La Prairie. It isn't like the wheat prairies in Alberta and Saskatchewan, it's simply the name of a place, a town, another small town, perhaps a nostalgic reminder of some happier times in the west. The Main, Saint Lawrence Main. Rue St Laurence, pronounced 'roo san loron'. A small variation in accent and stress, but it makes all the difference. It's everything. The thing is, the thing is . . . I wanted that child.

He could have been a farm boy from Chicoutimi or Yamachichi or some dead little fishing village on the Gaspé. She could have been from Peterborough or Pakenham, fleeing the pool-room corner, the taint of incest, the spectre of the laundromat every Tuesday and Thursday afternoon.

They could have met in the check-out line of Quatre Frères on a Saturday morning. He could have watched her struggling with her garbage bags, down the spiralling iron staircase one slippery winter morning as the dump truck lumbered past on rue Ste Famille. The aptly-named, the ironically-named 'roosanfamie': a short, quiet, tree-lined street that runs north from Sherbrooke to the seminary beside the park. Too narrow to be a throughway, it's packed with tiny houses jammed against each other for warmth, propping each other up so there isn't a gap for the high-rises to squeeze in.

She could live on a second-floor walk-up. Second, if you call the ground the first floor, which they do in Canada.

She could be Westmount-born, with muscular thighs from a childhood of riding and swimming and tennis lessons in outdoor courts, home from a few years' studying abroad. London or Paris. The Sorbonne, the LSE. Perhaps even Oxbridge, on a Rhodes.

She is still confused sometimes by terms like first- and second-floor. She uses words like 'flat' instead of 'apartment', 'rubbish' instead of 'garbage'. Sometimes slipping into her *français de la France* she speaks of *'le weekend'* or *'la waitress'* or *'Stop!'* Then he patiently points out that the Académie Québécoise has decreed the proper word to be *'la fin de semaine'*, *'la serveuse'* or *'Arrêt!'* He does this wryly, self-mockingly, but she notices as time goes on that he does it, he continues to do it, he does it increasingly as time goes on. He doesn't stop (*Arrêt!*).

Driving along the highway there are games you can play with yourself. ('Highway' is another of the words that sometimes slips away. The motorway. The boot of the car. The bonnet is open. The petrol tank is almost empty.) You can go so fast the broken white line joins up to make a barrier, an invisible wall to protect you from the other side, to prevent the other side from crossing over into your space. You can evolve relationships with the man in the car behind you. You pass him; he passes you. You smile at him in the rear-view mirror. You flash as he passes to let him know it's safe to slide in front. You speed up to tease him, testing him to see how far he will exceed the speed limit simply to stop you from getting ahead of him.

What's his hurry? Why is he driving so fast? So slowly? Does he have a wife to go home to? Is that why he's dawdling, fooling around on the highway with you? Is he speeding off to his mistress? With a car like that, is he a neurosurgeon or a travelling salesman?

Sometimes you find yourself riding eighty, ninety, a hundred miles an hour. It's a problem with these new cars: the air doesn't rush in with a roar around your head reminding you that you're hurtling through space. They're so well insulated you can forget there is a world out there beyond the thin skin of this car. It can pick up speed without you even noticing: eighty, ninety, one hundred miles an hour.

It's so easy to get diverted, a moment's inattention and suddenly you're off the main road. Suddenly you find yourself cruising down a slip road, 120 k's in a 50 k zone and the curve is rising up around you.

Diversions, that's the real danger. And speed. And roads *per se*. You're used to driving in miles per hour, you've just come back from a few years in England. Miles you understand; kilometres seem racy, fast, foreign. You can never work them out properly. And then there's the other guy on the road. That's the real variable; the missing figure in the equation so you can never know the final score.

'Objects in mirror are nearer than they appear.'

He could be one of the intelligentsia, bred in Laval or U de M in the sixties when Vatican II was releasing people from the Cure's grip, when *'Vive le Québec Libre'* could make spines tingle and no lines had been laid down yet. After Laval he studied Politics or Economics at the Sorbonne or the LSE and spoke English with a flawless vocabulary and a charmingly languid accent which had the girls in London smiling in their sleep. But back home in Quebec he spoke his native language and campaigned for Bill 101 which demanded that the children of immigrants be educated only in French.

Language Lessons.
English words to designate French Canadians:
Pepsi because it contained two more ounces per bottle than Coke for the same price, so the impoverished French Canadians drank it in quantity.

Pommes frites because they ate fried potatoes with everything: cheap food, easily grown on the farm or in the backyard.
Habitant often shortened to 'Hab', it's sort of French for pioneer.
Frogs, an honorary allusion to their European origins; it's unlikely that French Canadians eat more frogs than English Canadians; indeed they probably eat fewer.

A French child's language lesson: *maudit anglais*.

Let's say they met in the queue (line) for Cinema Parallel or the Théâtre du Nouveau Monde or the Place des Arts for Sunday morning *son et brioche*, they were bi-lingual, multi-cultural, urban sophisticates: interested, open – 'No sweat/*pas de problème*'. They entered into a relationship in the last rays of the evening sun that warmed the spot on the wooden floor through her back window.

'We're blessed,' he said.

'*Nous nous sommes rencontrés dans le sourire de Dieu,*' she said. (It was only later when words started crumbling around her that she realized that the French word for smile, *sourire*, was composed of *sous* and *rire*: 'under laugh', which could have sinister connotations: the low laugh, the snigger, the person laughing behind his/her hand.)

But at the beginning it was all *coeurs* and *fleurs* and *joie de vivre*. They were born of the same nation within a few miles of each other. It was that calm hiatus in the city's history; abortion had been accepted, the girls in the U de M hadn't yet been rounded up and gunned down by the madman: 'You feminists! See what you've done to me!'

Is there a cross on every hill in this country? R asked. She was showing him the city from the top of Mount Royal at night. She'd seen the view a hundred times but what never failed to impress her was the river, a black, velvet ribbon threading through the mass of neon twinkling below them. What impressed him was the neon: 'Trust Royale?' he asked. 'I would have thought Québécois would be the last to espouse monarchist slogans.'

It's a bank, she explained. It used to be called the Royal Trust. Because of the new language laws they have to translate it into French. (And so an insignificant dive known as Irv's place becomes Place d'Irv though history doesn't record whether the ladies of the night who frequent it are called hors d'oeuvres.)

Trust Royale. It must have been changed while she was in England. 'You'll render yourselves dumb with discretion,' he muttered, as the city's banks branded their names into the night sky: 'Alliance'; the intertwined initials which symbolized the 'Canadian Imperial Bank of Commerce'; 'BNE' – *Banque de Nouvelle-Ecosse:* New Scotland.

All the lines and squiggles, passing under the rhythmic eye of the searchlight from the top of the Place Ville Marie ('Place Vile Mary').

What really intrigued him was the cross: an international city still presided over by a cross. She told him how freshmen engineers shimmied up the cross each autumn to change the bulbs to spell 'Fuck Off'. It's a story everybody knows and tells and everybody knows someone who has seen or done it. But in all her years in the city she'd never actually seen it done. She doesn't tell him this.

She tells him about the cross on the far side of the slow, rocky river she watched from the bathroom window as she brushed her teeth in her grandmother's house every summer in her childhood.

She tells him about the broken stone cross on her grandmother's grave in the Protestant cemetery on the far side of the mountain which is separated from the Catholic cemetery by a barbed-wire fence, though oddly enough the Jewish cemetery lies alongside it, encroaching year by year without any hint of a barrier. The city has a strong Jewish lobby.

And as they slip back down the mountain, through the late-night rustlings, through the cruisers still madly pursuing their thrills, she explains that the favourite pick-up spot is right under the cross. All the inverts and outcasts make their way up here, to find a bit of warmth in the glow of the cross at the top of the mountain in the middle of the night.

When she's finished her tour he pulls out the question: 'Why?'

She doesn't tell him about the Frenchman who liked to correct her vocabulary.

'Why do you keep coming back to this country?'

Perhaps some people have a landscape. Perhaps this one is mine, she says, sweeping her arm across the North Shore, the headlands, the cold, grey river, the hills rising up from the rocks, yellow with mustard grass, purple with bishop's weed, blue with clover and vetch and cornflower and a dozen shades of green.

She tries to explain about her country.

Mon pays, ce n'est pas un pays, c'est un . . . what?
Mon pays ce n'est pas une . . .
What is the line, the line from that song?
Mon pays ce n'est pas un pays c'est de la neige . . .
My country is not a country, it's snow.

You were happy in England, weren't you?

How to explain the lure of the one who rejected you.

Have you heard of a man called Morgenthaler? she asks.
'The name is vaguely familiar.'
He fought for abortions. He invented a suction technique. Simple, quick, you queue in the waiting room – no anaesthetic, no overnight stays, no train rides out to discreet country houses masquerading as rest cures. You

lie on the table, open your legs – whoosh – it sucks out the unwanted cells.

'Yes. And?'

That's all. That's it. Over and done with. You ring for an appointment like a facial or a pedicure. A couple of hours and you're back on the streets as though nothing has happened.

'Why are you telling me this?'

She shrugs.

'I want you to come home,' he says.

I am home.
This isn't your home.

By this time they are walking along the plateau. This area is called the student ghetto, she explains. Though there aren't many students left any more. A ghetto of doctors and lawyers. In my day people spent the summer evenings gossiping on their front steps. Every alley had cats and bag ladies and people jamming Dylan and Lennon and Cohen songs.

'That time has passed. You no longer belong here.'

I know.

Thinking about it later she realized that the plaque at the top of the mountain was gone. It had been taken down to be replaced by a more precise plaque which would read: 'Mount Royal (English) was discovered by Jacques Cartier (French) who was led here by the Indians (Native Peoples) who were drawn here by the nuts . . .'

He had a suite at the Ritz. He'd booked a single room but the hotel was empty so they'd upgraded him. He didn't know any hotels in the city so he went for a name he recognized. He knew it would please her. She still took a childish pleasure in hotels.

The Montreal Ritz was the one hotel in her life that didn't disappoint. The upstairs corridors were as elegant and polished as the foyer. Even the sand in the ashtrays was stamped with the Ritz crest.

She had met him at the airport. She hadn't intended to stay with him but when she saw the room it was a shame to waste all that space. She could chalk it up with all the other hotels: the Plaza, the Pierre, the Algonquin, the Chelsea. The Berkeley, the Connaught, the Savoy, the Dorchester, Claridges, Browns. The Cipriani, the Danielli. The George V. The Infanta de Sangres. Plus all the other hotels whose names she had forgotten. And her favourite hotel of all, the tiny *pensione* with the vine-covered veranda overlooking the Arno where she had spent her honeymoon a hundred years before.

The Ritz. A suite at the Ritz overlooking the garden. Somewhere, floors below, there was probably a patch of green, but you couldn't see it from that height. 'I'm afraid the garden is closed for renovation,' the porter explained. Breakfast with the ducks, she remembered. It was something her grandmother used to do. One of the stories from her childhood. 'The ducks are taking a sabbatical,' he consoled. 'But the room is very peaceful.' He was a saint. The name embroidered on his breast was Matthew or Mark. Or Luke or John. Or maybe it was Anthony: St Anthony, the patron saint of lost things. His hair was long at the sides, bald on top: a tonsure – from '*tondre*': 'to shear, clip, to cut'. Does this imply eunuchs? she wondered. His face was serene and angelic. Perhaps he was indeed above sex; sex, desire, the whole bloody thing. He slid round the room like a nurse or a monk.

'Must be a quota employee,' R muttered when the porter glided into the bathroom to switch on the lights, to check the taps, the towels, the toiletries. She giggled. They giggled together. They giggled a lot. She and the Frenchman hadn't giggled much. They'd discussed. They'd explained. He had explained; she had listened.

St Anthony wafted round the room touching buttons, opening doors and drawers and cupboards: the safe, the fridge, the TV, the radio, the extra pillows, blankets, beds, the air conditioning, the heating, the panic button.

Pulling back the curtains he brandished the view like a banner: 'And the windows really open.'
I suppose you don't have many suicides here, she commented.
St Anthony hesitated a moment, then, as though he hadn't heard, he cut short his tour and bowed his way backwards out of the room.

I want him, she whispered.

'Pervert,' he chuckled, wrapping his arms around her.

I want that serenity, she replied. I want, I want, I want to know where to find things.

This city. Ben's, Schwartz's, Sammy's. He was surprised to see the Hassidic children playing in the street on rue Ste Famille. It's a city of many cultures, she said.

The shops: Arahova, Smolensky, Lee Ho Yun.

The flags: the red maple leaf, the blue fleur de lis. Count them on Sherbrooke Street, on rue St Catherine: two maple leafs, two fleurs de lis. The Bay (*La Baie*) is hedging its bets; two maple leafs, one, two, three fleurs de lis: the Bay is casting its vote with the French. Eaton's is going with the flow, one of each flag: diplomacy reigns.

What can I tell you? This is a story, that's all. An Englishman's weekend in Montreal. Mount Royal. Mon tree all. Montree all. Mon treal. He wants to go to the art gallery: Le Musée des Beaux Arts. He is a connoisseur of paintings. She likes to move so close to the canvas that the images dissolve and all she can see are the brush strokes, the colour and texture and length of the lines. The warp and the weft of the canvas pushing through the paint, asserting themselves with time.

She liked the painting of the poor people jammed into the cheap seats, straining over the barrier, faces glowing in the limelight, enchanted by the circus unfolding miles below them. He likes the portraits: Rembrandts. She never understood the appeal, though she knows that portraits are said to be the highest form of art. She prefers pictures that tell stories: chaos, colour, crowd scenes, not the discreet gaze of a single face, obscuring all the drama.

What we're talking about here is just seven, maybe eight city blocks: rue St Denis to Mountain Street. We're talking about a very small space.

Sometimes, when driving down the highway, she imagined veering just slightly into the oncoming lane. She could imagine the impact, the crash, the car twisting, spinning, smashed into again by the traffic behind her. The bang, the crash, the car spinning round like a dodgem car at the fairground, glass everywhere and the spines of metal poking up like spears, like elbows out of their sockets, poking up through skin.

The trick in driving is to remember what's behind you. Watch what's in front, of course, but never forget what's following, what's coming upon you from the back.

This is important, she said. I'm trying to explain myself to you, to make you understand. Spaces are part of one's psyche. Long distances must somehow be traversed. Endless drives down highways at night.

Techniques for staying awake while driving:

1. Open all the windows in the winter. In summer too, but it isn't so effective.

2. Turn the radio on high; if possible find a pop station and sing along with the songs. Words are always better than music. Try to find some talking: an interview programme, a problem phone-in. Music deceives. Mozart,

Bach and Chopin are especially bad: too regular, they blend with the lines in the road and lull you to sleep. If you have to have music choose Liszt or Stravinsky or Wagner if you can stand him.

3. Hyperventilate. Remember at school when you used to do this in the playground competing to see who could faint the fastest – Darleen Donolly always won. You're not the sort to take it all the way; you haven't the courage. Nonetheless, beware of going too far; stop when you start feeling happy.

4. In the absence of a pea of sufficient size, stick your shoe or boot behind your back so it pokes into you; the irritation should keep you tossing, and there's also the added benefit of a slowly freezing foot to prevent you from drifting off to sleep.

5. Talk to yourself. Count out loud if all other forms of conversation fail. Recite poems (I'llnotocarrioncomfort despair), hymns, prayers, the Bible/Talmud/Koran, a hundred bottles of beer on the wall, whenever I walk on a London street I'm ever so careful to watch my feet etc.

6. Keep your brights on so the oncoming traffic will flash and honk and curse you in passing.

7. Think carefully before picking up hitchers. Despite your vows and promises and bargains with God all those sweltering afternoons on the tarmac of the Route Nationale or the Autoroute du Midi or the M1 or the Trans Canada or the Mass Pike you are older now, you have become one of those people you used to curse as they breezed past you with their empty cars and apologetic shrugs.

She looked for his reflection everywhere, in every window, in every passing subway train or car, in every crowd. She was convinced that he was watching her from somewhere. At parties, with strangers, she'd laugh especially loud, she'd dress with care and elegance and make more effort than she ever had in London, simply so the word would reach him that she was back in the city.

She would smile mysteriously or toss her head around or chuckle to herself while walking down an empty street. In cafés she'd assume pretty poses and pretend to read *La Presse, Le Monde, Le Devoir* and occasionally *Le Canard Enchaîné:* the enchained duck, like the ducks on sabbatical in the Ritz garden.

She returned to all the places they used to go, taking the Englishman with her as a talisman. Of course he can't possibly be there, she reasoned to herself, pulling the Englishman to certain cafés, certain cinemas and grocery shops. With two days in the city he couldn't understand why she suddenly wanted to visit the Quatre Frères deli, the Cinema Parallel, the Théâtre du Nouveau Monde. He only had two days in the city; he'd come all this way to see her and she was insisting on all these silly errands.

Let me tell you a story, she said, as they waited in the foyer for the limousine to take him away. I had a friend once, who had a lover – we'll say he was a different race, colour, creed, perhaps a different class; perhaps the difference between them came down to a few city blocks.

She adored him; he pursued her, he was her Dark Montrealer, he buried his hidden hook deep into her flesh, he caught her, hauled her in, netted her. But once he had her he wasn't quite sure . . . He was happy to spend his day and nights with her behind closed doors, but when they went out in the streets he would keep his hands plunged firmly in his pockets. Occasionally he'd hold a door open for her, but he never put his arm around her and he flinched whenever she demonstrated affection towards him in public.

It wasn't a social embarrassment; it came down to politics really. He liked the way she spoke, he liked her language, her vocabulary, her accent. It was the proper accent. But what he liked most was when she tried to speak his language, because then he could correct her. And that's what he liked most of all.

'Why are you telling me this?' he asked as they waited for the car to take him back to England.

Wait, the story isn't finished; you haven't heard the punchline. She stroked his hand to calm him down. He had no problem with public displays of affection.

Eventually, after days and nights in a room with this man, she got pregnant. She, of course, was delighted.
'How did the man feel about it?' he asked.

St Anthony was motioning: the airport limo had arrived.

He didn't know, she replied. She was going to tell him, she continued. She hadn't missed St Anthony's mime, she could see he was getting anxious. She didn't want to distress St Anthony: you never know when you might become lost and need someone to find you.

She fully intended to tell him, she explained, but he was killed before she could. Killed on the highway, driving from Montreal to Quebec late one night. A stranger came up behind, passed too close beside him, pushed him off the highway; car rolled over into the river. The other guy just kept on driving.

They found the body three weeks later, floating, bloated, trapped in the weeds several miles down the river, guarded by two herons. Two blue herons, she added. Blue herons are rare this far north, they are a southern bird. They usually nest in places like Brazil, like Rio de Janeiro – she pulled out the 'Janeiro', into three distinct, elongated syllables, as though the word itself could mask the image that it was being used to forestall. Nobody knows what the herons were doing in the St Lawrence River that year.

And that's the end of the story, she said, leading him to the limo that was idling anxiously in the traffic, waiting to take him away.

But the thing is, she leaned through the open window to give him one last embrace.

The thing is, she drew his face to her lips.
The thing is, I really can't believe, she whispered into his ear.
I really cannot bring myself to believe that he isn't still here, somewhere.

She was searching. Always searching.
She never found what she was searching for.
He knew that if he waited long enough she would return to London, if not, indeed, to him.

24 Crossing the Frontier

The things that are lost are the things one remembers most: the unanswered questions, the conversations that never occurred, the missed encounters.

It rained all night in Porto after we arrived. I woke at dawn that first morning and through the shutters thought I heard the military marching in the streets: the regular drumming, the slightly muzzy echo. 'They're coming to get you,' R teased when I told him. (Yes, I'm back with him again.) It was just the rain beating on the tin roof and the church bells marking time.

We rented the car in the city and were travelling up the port rivers trying to exorcize one crisis or another. I suppose it was another love affair. Another unsuccessful love affair. I suppose it was my love affair that we were exorcizing. R was my protector. When everything else crumbled I would return to him.

That particular day we decided to drive into Spain. It was his idea. A change of plan. A whim. I think he was getting bored with me, and Portugal in the rain, and the endless succession of trim little valleys glimpsed from the car through the downpour. Perhaps he was trying to jerk me from the tears, the depression, the lethargy with a change of scene.

By midday the ubiquitous rain had become a freak storm: hail and snow, all the roads were running like rivers, the eucalyptus trees were like a solid curtain of silver beside us. The frontier was a hut at the top of the pass. A grey stone hut, barely visible. It looked like it hadn't seen human life in a hundred million years.

Suddenly someone rushed out and flagged us down. We were led from the car, through the rain, into the building, by an irritated young man in an oilskin. I don't suppose he expected to be disturbed, but having been, he was determined to disturb us in return. He demanded our passports then disappeared behind a thick wooden door.

We stood there, dripping on the threshold, peering into this cavernous room with a fire blazing at the far end. Three wooden chairs were drawn up round it although there was only the one man in evidence.

On the wall behind us was a map of the region faded to sepia, obscuring most of the place names we'd passed: 1930s judging from the typeface; it had that upright unadorned, black type reminiscent of the Nazis.

As soon as we settled into the chairs the man returned, threw down our passports and motioned to us to go. What about a stamp? I asked. It's not that one ever reads them, not that one can decipher the marks or relate them to this or that trip, but having a passport full of border stamps makes me feel I've been somewhere.

The man sighed, shrugged, disappeared again with the passports, returning a few minutes later, giving us just enough time to relax without actually getting warm.

Leafing through the passports as we waited for the deluge to pass in a bar in Spain, I noticed that he'd stamped the 3rd of March, though it was already the 6th.

Thinking back on it now it's odd perhaps that I knew the date. Weeks can pass where I've no idea of the date or day, but the 6th of March I know because it was the day of my abortion two weeks before, the date of my wedding ten years before. (Days. Dates. By these random details we eke out significance, seeking some meaning in coincidence.)

A landscape over the Douro: R was photographing a terraced hillside. Despite the rain I stepped out of the car into a field full of wild flowers: purple and yellow and white. It reminded me of a photo of me lying in the grass like Ophelia when my husband and I drove to Italy on our honeymoon.

Photographs I wish I had taken that trip – like things on antique stalls in village squares you'll never find again or clothes you tried on once in a shop in Paris and regret not having bought ever since:

1. A lemon tree in front of a blue house: the waxy green leaves, the fluorescent yellow orbs of fruit, the bright blue of the wall behind.
2. A slate-blue house with apple-green shutters; the chalky pastels, blue and green, which decorate this countryside.
3. An almond tree in blossom, against a crumbling whitewashed wall. The pink-tinged petals, the black lines of the branches, the white of the background: a Japanese etching; a memento mori.

Shapes, colours, smells. The pleasure of travel. All decisions are external: which way to go, when, where, what to eat. The mind is preoccupied with sensations: architecture, landscape. The fruit trees. The grape vines. The ironwork, stonework, the mosses, the brands of bottled beer or water.

Driving back through the forest the smell of eucalyptus reminds me of a drive through a forest in Umbria ten years before: my honeymoon; the Ophelia photo. That journey invades me now, even though it was so long ago.

R and me. How do they see us? An older man, a younger woman? A classic story? It looks simple enough. In truth, it is the story of a man taking a woman off to recover after her abortion of another man's child. Didn't I explain that before? The love affair, the unsuccessful love affair, what I was attempting to exorcize is what I'd already aborted. 'Terminate' I believe is the word they use at the clinic.

You have to choose the object of your affections with more care.

I kiss R. Remark on how relaxed he is about kissing in public.

And at night, when it's all falling apart, I cry quietly, curled in my corner. He inches over, puts his arm around me: 'It will be all right, baby. You'll get your life together. Everybody loves you,' he murmurs.
Not the aborted child.

What does one wear to an abortion?
Jeans? You don't want to look too defiant. Look suitably chaste; a victim, not a slut. But don't appear too vulnerable; victims invite contempt, abuse; you don't want them to botch up the job. Try to appear competent. Confident. See it as a stroke of bad luck. Smile wryly: 'Betrayed by biology.' Give it a Woody Allen spin; crack a joke for the anaesthetist; he must – yes, of course it's a he – he must get pretty bored with the endless procession of haggard women looking guilty, looking scared.

Be wry, but not cheery; this is a solemn occasion. 'This is murder. You'll regret it for the rest of your life!' the woman outside the clinic cried, pawing you as you hurried inside.

But a serious skirt and sweater seems like a costume, like a fraud; after all, they know you 'Did It', you 'Made Love'. No, not 'Love'; what you made was . . . What? A foetus? Not even that; a mucus-like collection of cells, smaller than the head of a biro. It was, now it isn't.

So, still the perennial problem . . . Decent trousers, not too expensive. It's lousy work for them at the clinic, only attracts the hard-up doctors, the Indian and African nurses, women whose colour bars them from the gleaming, white wards of a less discreet nature. Don't arouse their envy; after all, what you're paying for a night's unchecked passion is probably more than they make in a week.

The landscape in Spain: as soon as you cross the border the land becomes hard and brown. The vines are neglected, overgrown, woody and dying. The ground heaves with rocks. The landscape jars. I don't like this place, I say; let's go back now.

R is slow to answer. The place appeals to him. 'Being a soft person, I find it a contrast. You being so hard, prefer softer surroundings. But he concedes and after one drink in a bar, during which we examine the passports and discover the mistaken date, we turn round and make our way back to Portugal.

Can you photograph a rainbow? R and I discuss this one morning driving through the rain. Somehow it seems the rainbow, the sun, the break in the storm always occurs on the far side of the valley. R thinks if something is visible it can be photographed. I think that since it is an optical illusion it won't show up on film. He stops the car, I take the test photo, looking back across the valley, struggling to keep the lens dry without blocking out the view. It's only later that I remember it's a black and white film. Later still, the camera is stolen, so I'll never know.

The rainbow is a symbol of forgiveness, reconciliation; it was God's sign after the flood. Is it significant, I wonder, that the rainbow occurs several valleys behind me?

I read from the guide book as R drives. The Lima River in Northern Portugal, one of the great Port rivers: you have to imagine the graceful, double-ended boats, like vast gondolas, slipping down the current, sliding their barrels of wine from the quiet, rolling vineyards down to the bustle and stink of the port.

The Romans thought the Lima was the Lethe, River of Oblivion. They sent their bravest general to wade across the current. He had to call each man by name to convince the troops that he wasn't forgetting, that he hadn't slipped into oblivion, that the river was safe to cross.

Today the Lima is a tiny, shallow, not particularly pretty stream. I can't imagine why they would think it was the Lethe. R can't imagine either, though he is not seeking oblivion. In any case, the Lima River in Northern Portugal is not the place to find it.

R asks me if I want to drive. I've forgotten my licence. I'm reluctant to take the risk. I feel my luck is running thin. These days I can't imagine climbing into the driver's seat ever again. This feeling will pass. Feelings aren't facts.

He repeats the question: 'Why don't you take the wheel while I navigate for a while?' I don't tell him I've forgotten my licence. I've done it before, recently, with him. He'll think it's not chance. Nothing is chance. Nothing is random. Everything has a reason, he says. He is wrong. Some things simply are. I don't explain this to him. He's better at arguing than I am; I suspect he would win a discussion on the matter. It is a feeling I have. Some things simply are: feelings, not facts.

I say all right, pull over. I climb out of the car. I walk around the front of it: 'Beware of oncoming traffic.' The engine steams slightly in the drizzle. The gravel crunches underfoot. Black, greasy stones: in isolation each one could be beautiful, en masse you barely notice them. I open the door on the driver's side. He slides across, into the passenger seat.

'Signal your intentions clearly. Don't turn on your indicators till you are prepared to act, you'll only confuse the driver behind. You might even cause an accident.' I was taught this by a stranger on a night drive from London to Paris. We left Calais at midnight, arrived at the Ile de la Cité just as dawn was breaking. I'd managed to stay awake the whole journey.

It's amazing how quickly one forgets the finer details of road safety.

I am in Portugal in the rain. It could be anywhere, but it's here, in this room shaped like a slice of cake. 'A slice of pie,' I describe it to R but he says: 'In England we'd say "cake".' We aren't in England, but we might as well be.

Rain keeps everything inside. The ceiling is peeling. White plaster. A fifties wardrobe of cheap stained wood; the glue has stopped sticking. Over the largest crack in the wall is a garish print: women in gardens: Marie Antoinette. This is not the tourist season. We are the only guests in the hotel. It is an old hunting lodge. I ask the man at the desk how old the place is.

'Very old,' he replies, proud of his English.

How old? I repeat.

'Opened nineteen forty,' he beams.

I know it opened in nineteen forty, I read the brochure, but when was it built?

'Very old. Nineteen forty. Fifty years,' he smiles politely.

Perhaps he knows I come from the New World where fifty years is considered old. The building could be nineteenth-century; it could be much earlier. I don't know enough about architecture. I want to know how old it is. The man doesn't know the answer, he doesn't understand the question.

Tomorrow morning we will leave this place. Three minutes after we've gone, two minutes, we won't be able to see it. The grey cloud is everywhere. An hour down the highway I will have forgotten all about it, except for the man and his bland smile. Perhaps if he'd told me the date of the place, I would have forgotten the journey completely.

Weeks later with R – or with somebody else – in London or Montreal or Madrid, I will struggle to remember: where did we spend that night, remind me? The room? The view? The other guests?

'We were alone, the only ones. The man at the desk was from Mozambique.'

But he wasn't black, I will protest; I'm sure I would remember if he had been.

'He was a settler. His family had been there for three generations. After the Independence they left, they returned to Portugal. Although they'd lived in Mozambique for three generations, they were afraid of the Independence, so they returned to a country they'd never known.'

'There was a fire in the dining room when we arrived,' he will add. Then I will remember: when we went down to dinner the fire had burned out. The man put two logs on the embers but they never took.

And the meal? I will ask.

'The meal was the meal we had every day; green soup: '*calde verde*'. Grilled fish. Fried potatoes. Rice, good rice. And tomatoes which really taste of tomato.'

. . . And a thin sparkling wine which, however rich and deep the colour, always tasted thin and bitter.

And pudding: a yellow brown flan, the texture and taste of wallpaper paste.

Everyone said the food would be excellent. It wasn't. But in years to come when somebody tells me they're going to Portugal I will say: oh the food there is excellent, so fresh and clean and the sparkling green wines.

And you must drive along the Lima; one of the great port rivers of Portugal. The Lima, the Lethe, the River of Oblivion.

Perhaps I should simply settle with R.

Over dinner, over sherry and wine and Cointreau and whisky, over candles and linen and discreet music and the soft bubble of laughter and chat from the couples sitting behind and beside you, people's lives sound so neat and easy: the affair, the discovery, the break-down, the break-up, the adjustment, the terms, the divorce. And now the new wedding date: cause for a fond disagreement, a cheerful declaration of one's total servitude to the newly beloved, the newly to have and to hold from this day forth in sickness forever etcetera.

Between the *amuse-gueules* and the *pousse café*, the tiny tiff, the 'darling you mustn't just a small one you won't sleep I will you won't have a whisky instead no I'm driving I'll drive . . .' when the waiter glides up with the bill on a plate and everyone pauses a moment, like the moment the ambulance passes, everyone pauses, suspended, a moment, wondering who will pay . . .

25 Saffron

I am in Morocco, packing to go home. I have promised to get some saffron for my mother but I can't find any. I'm in a hurry, I keep running into these stalls, I can see it there, the tiny cellophane packages glistening like honey, flickering like butterflies, shining on the dark back walls of the dingy stalls.

But the men keep hiding it just as I approach, shaking their heads: oh no no no, they say. They say they are out of saffron, or there isn't any left, or they aren't that type of shop. But I know it is there, I see it gleaming, the yellow powder. Gold. And the cellophane is covered in dust. Not the inside, but the outside of the package, so it isn't even that the men are keeping it for someone else. It's just sitting there, getting dusty, getting old.

But they won't give it to me, lend it, sell it, barter it. And I'm desperate, desolate that I will disappoint my mother. If I don't find it soon I will miss the plane home.

You're getting old. You can't keep playing about like this, fucking around, messing up, wasting time time time.

It's all fading, sagging, wrinkling; it's all sifting away, it's all slipping from your grasp. And yet. And yet.

Mum I couldn't get it.
Mum I didn't forget, I tried I really did.
Mum I really wanted to find it for you, it was there; I know it was, it was just within my grasp. Nearly. Almost. Almost but not quite.

But saffron doesn't come from Morocco, it comes from Spain.

Yes, I know; that's part of the problem.
Morocco is just where I happened to be.
Morocco is where you were gutted.
I keep on going back there.

You see the men keep denying it. They're holding it back.
Buy some from the women.
There are no women in the market places – only cripples and whores.
The women peer from their high latticed windows through their black veils – the long hooked nose an eagle's beak, a hawk, circling patiently waiting for the prey to tire before diving in for the kill.

I keep on looking in the wrong place. Going back and going back to the same wrong place. But I know how much you want it. Need it. Saffron. Your supply is running out. How will you colour and spice your paellas without saffron? How will you paint your kitchen walls that sunny yellow? How will you lighten your days in that dark kitchen without the saffron that I can't seem to find anymore.

Shall we grow our own crocuses, in neat rows in the garden, an army of crocuses marching down the lawn? And when they unfurl, slowly, in the morning, as the sun's rays caress them, the slender shafts of light just touching their buds, just teasing them to open, we will seize that moment, just before the peak, just before the climax and then we will harvest.

We will patrol our army, just you and me, Mum. We'll step out each morning at dawn with our brushes to dust off the stamens, to capture the essence, to preserve that powder. Just you and me, Mum. We'll harvest that powder, save it from waste. From casual destruction by insects and animals rushing past. From unknowing winds simply sweeping it off. From somebody else with their own early brush sneaking our powder before it is ripe. From the waste of simply growing old without having ever been gathered, collected, the powder drying like the magic on butterflies' wings as they age.

The precise powder of the butterfly's wing, the saffron-like powder. Careful: if you touch it the butterfly won't be able to fly anymore. Grounded; on earth it will die.

As the butterfly ages, the powder dries up, wisping off, drifting away. And each grain that goes the wings are brought lower, closer to the ground. Till the butterfly is left flapping, at the top of a bookcase, on a high window ledge, in a dark crevice of the cold, summer fireplace, trapped in a spider's web, naked and gasping in a corner on the floor. Fluttering, aimless, waiting, waiting simply for the end.

Till the dog, intrigued, consumes it, with one quick, unsatisfactory snap. Or your mother, despite your protests, crushes it with a flash of her sole, grinds it to powder: wisp, like the crackle of dried leaves in autumn. It was almost dead anyway, it was dying. Then the hoover sucks the dust away and the butterfly is gone. Disappeared. A mere memory.

Butterfly: a symbol of the Resurrection. Often found in paintings of the Virgin and Child, usually in the Child's clenched fist.
The butterfly's significance derives from the three stages of its life – caterpillar, chrysalis and butterfly – which can be seen to symbolize life, death and resurrection.

Saffron: from Arab 'zafaran' meaning 'yellow'.
Yellow, the colour of happiness, colour of thought.
Yellow, the colour of cowards, of fear.

26 My Wife and I Have an Arrangement

He walks into a room and you think Oh God Oh no Oh not again. You've heard of this man: 'He's so . . . He does . . . He is . . .' And you vowed, even then, even before you knew him you vowed that you wouldn't . . . But here he is. And you haven't even met. And still you know that this will be, this will have to be . . .

A conference. You have been here before. A man walked in . . . But at the last moment he withdrew, as it were; he pulled out, leaving you cap in hand, standing at the door: the sanctity of marriage. And so a fidelity of sorts was preserved.

But that was several lives ago when you were also still a wife.

He sits down opposite you at the table. He smiles. You turn and talk talk talk to the man on your left, the man on your right, you don't even look at him, you catch his eye in passing and quickly turn away and all that afternoon you avoid him in the garden, in the conference room, in the cafeteria. But evening comes and you're seated again, eating again, and he enters, late, again. And again he sits down and smiles, three places down on the far side of the table. And again you glance away.

He sits, so easy, so sure of his place. He takes off his jacket, the green braces flash, the polka-dot tie. And you pray, oh please God, no, not again.

You can't keep careening . . . You must break this pattern. Still you find yourself looking for clues: A ring? No. The watch? Yes, a fluorescent plastic watch, well of course he would have children. A man like this, of course he would be married. And so you turn away. But that polka-dot tie has burned into your brain.

Later, after the coffee and brandy, after the speeches and the mocking asides, after the final thanks and the applause, when everyone's finally filing away, you stand, laughing, on the edge of another group and he hurries over and pulls you aside.

I don't know who you are.

So you talk, of course, and the room empties quietly, smiling, discreetly. The lights dim and he gestures you to a sofa: America, Pop Art, the Censorship Debate. All very, all quite . . . Till the janitors come to sweep you away.

And out in the night the lights have all died and the buses are sleeping so of course he has to drive you back to your hotel. But of course you neither of you know the way. Later he will say when you offer to drive him to Brighton for the night, he will pause for a moment and answer, yes, it would be very nice, I haven't been driven in ages, and I'd be honoured to be driven by you. But that is still several weeks in the future. Tonight it is he who is driving you. And you are still vowing to protect yourself.

You get lost in the unlit streets of this seedy seaside resort. This is it, you think, now I've blown any chance: he's a busy man, he's a man in a hurry, he hasn't time to drive me around. Now I've delayed him here all night, preventing him from returning to his waiting wife and children. But you're damned if you're going to apologize, and of course it is in that simple vow that you are, indeed, damned.

You find a place. This will do, you say, I can walk from here. He pulls over, opens the door. That's it. A flash.

Your eyes. The hook. It slips. The quick jerk to make sure it's taken. You pull away with a very tiny, barely audible, breezy, casual, 'thanks'.
For?
The lift.
Fine, he says and he's gone, leaving you in front of the wrong hotel in the pit of the night.

But you walk and walk.

If you keep on going in the same direction you have to get somewhere eventually. The trick is not to deviate or you may turn back on yourself without knowing, then you're lost forever.

And all that night and all the next day you think: is it . . . is it real? Is it simply me? But the amused, sympathetic smiles of the others suggest you have not made it up.

And suddenly he telephones:
Hello. It's me.

And so it begins.

I feel you're a black hole sucking me in.
It doesn't need to be like that . . . unless you want it to be.

I feel you're a black hole sucking me in.
And what do you intend to do about it?
Half of me longs to save you; half of me longs to save myself.
Which half will win?
I'm not much for resisting a challenge (especially one with self-destruction written all over it).

So it begins.

You know this scene. Bad politics. This is the one encounter you always swore . . . It isn't politics, not really, it's pragmatism: simple arithmetic. Nobody wins. And the one who loses most is always the Other Woman.

A marriage is like a pair of scissors, someone said: however far apart the blades seem they are still joined in the middle. And anyone who comes between them will get sliced in two.

What do you want with this man, this carapace of charm which hides the emptiness that is consuming him?

Why me? you say.
You're independent, attractive, quick-witted, we're few and far between.
– We: you and me.

He's grasping at straws. A drowning man grabbing a thin willow branch hanging out over the river. He's Solomon interviewing for a new virgin. He's Dracula looking for some fresh blood to keep him alive another day.
And let's be honest, he smiles disarmingly, you're sexy.

Why me? you ask another time.
You have a lot going for you, he replies. You're young. You have potential. You're independent.

Independent. Independent: the word keeps recurring: no strings, no connections. I know this refrain.

And what about . . . ?
My wife and I have an arrangement, he answers, before you even finish the question.

It's the perfect set-up, this, isn't it? You've made it all perfectly plain from the start: there is no chance of any involvement, just sex . . .
(the phrase echoes:
I'm just here for the sex
All I want is the sex
If that's not enough for you that's fine, just say and I'll go . . .)

You won't leave your wife and daughters, you stay together for the girls, you have separate lovers, you keep it discreet, it's all kosher, accepted, understood. No sweat.
Ah, he replies, drawing out the gauntlet . . . But you always hope that this will be the one that breaks the pattern.

So there it lies: the gauntlet, between you, gleaming in the dust: the soft white kid, slender as a reed. You long to slide it slowly over your palm, across your wrist, up your vulnerable arm; you long to leave it lying, neglected, in the dust.

You long to cut off each of the fingers and plant them one by one in the earth; a row of little kid fingers to water and weed through the long summer evenings, to harvest in autumn, a gift for your mother, a bouquet of little kid fingers, home-grown, by you, for her.

No: you long to blow the fingers into five helium balloons and release them in a bundle to sail across the city.

No: you long to use them as prophylactics, one each day for a working week, and then it will be over: all passion spent.

The first evening he arranges to meet: eight o'clock. Half past eight, nine o'clock, nine-fifteen. If he were keen he'd have arrived early.
Ten o'clock. Already you feel like a neglected wife and you aren't even lovers. Finally the bell goes.
The speeches:
Look, I'm clearly not cut out for this . . .
Already this is too reminiscent . . . I left all this sort of thing with my marriage . . .
I'll never be more than a convenience . . .
I'm used to having a greater impact . . .
I'm too proud . . .
I respect myself too much to be just . . .

But he walks in the door, a bunch of wilted flowers: anemones, 'an enemy' . . . And suddenly all the words evaporate.
Are you ready to go? I'm parked on a double-yellow.
So you do. Go. You do go.

Oh dear, he says, brushing the papers off the passenger seat, sweeping them randomly onto the floor.

Why 'oh dear'? you ask. As you are intended to ask.
Right on cue.
This is a bad beginning.
('Beginning': you note it, you note down the word.
Beginning implies a middle and an end, implies a whole story not a one-night-stand. Beginning implies a future.)
Women always complain about the mess that men make.
I'm sorry about all this . . . This car is a rolling rubbish tip. I'm terribly sorry.

A tip. A tip. This place is a shitheap, this place is a tip.

Look, do me a favour. Don't apologize.
Just one thing before we begin: don't ever say you're sorry. I spent ten years with a man who apologized to me daily, hourly, minutely. Apologizing is a way of not doing anything about it. Apologizing is an acceptance of the situation, not a promise to change it.
He looks, amused. He doesn't reply.

He doesn't look at you, he looks at the road, the papers, the mess in the back, the passing scene. He's the first man you've met who doesn't steal sidelong glances, who doesn't look at you in the face, the eyes. His eyes are always cast to the ground, the side, the ceiling, avoiding the hook.

And later that first evening, pouring the wine, you see his hand tremble and think: is it possible? Is he . . . could he be . . . ?
And later he drives you back to your flat and you notice him, swerving and jerking, and you noticed he hardly drank at all. Is this man, could he possibly be . . . nervous?

Anemone: in pagan mythology a symbol of sorrow and death. In the Greek legend Adonis died on a bed of anemones which turned from white to red with his blood. Often these flowers appear in depictions of the Crucifixion, or accompanying the Virgin to indicate her sorrow at the Passion. The triple leaf of the anemone sometimes symbolizes the Trinity.

The car purrs to a stop, then silence:
I never know what to do at this step.
At this step, he echoes: is this a step?
Of course it's a step: you know it, he knows it, a step on the journey to anguish – yours; to guilt, irritation, perhaps a little mild regret – his. But still you proceed.
You could invite me in for coffee.
Do you want a wine/whisky/coffee?
He smiles, nods.
And what then? you ask.
We wait and see. There are no rules from here on in. The one thing we can do is be honest. I promise I will be honest with you. If you ever have any questions . . . and you mustn't ever hesitate to ask.

Honesty. Honesty. Honesty is a dry white plant which rustles in the wind. Girls in long skirts gather it to keep in vases on their windowsills.

I don't want to do this, you whine as you climb on top of him, pinning him to the bed. Just say no. Just say no. Nancy implores you, grinning her corpse's First Lady grin. Nobody needs it. Be strong, be mature – maturity: ha! Deny the impulse: simply say no.

Ah, but do you have any choice? He taunts as you fill his mouth with your sorrows. Pull away if you like. If it's all too much for you. If this isn't what you want. You must do what you have to. Do what you think's best. If you can . . .

The thing is, the thing is: these things don't have a definite end.

You say to yourself, what the hell, I'll plunge in and ride it a while, since I can't seem to get anywhere anyway, since I haven't slept an hour or eaten a meal or opened a book since I met him five days ago.
You say: do I have any choice anyway?
Just say no.

All night you ask about his wife, his children, his past lovers. You know in the morning the ones you will envy most, the ones you will secretly rage against are the daughters.

What do you want with a man who is so far removed from himself? His voice is trapped in his throat like a bird. His walk is stiff: clipped and contained. He tells his stories, but when you break in with one of your own he listens politely, eyes vacant. And when you're finished he simply continues where he left off. No comment. As though you hadn't even spoken. As though he hadn't even heard.
He answers all your questions but he doesn't ask about you or your life.

Where does he live, this man? Where does he hang his skin at night?

I dreamed I was holding you, rocking you like Michelangelo's 'Pieta'. The tears were sliding down your face, wetting the front of my dress.
Did the dream explain why I was crying?
No, but it didn't matter. The point was, you were letting go and I was comforting you . . . I don't suppose that particular dream will ever come true . . .
No, I don't suppose it will. I do cry, you know – at concerts and films. I used to be able to cry at will. It was a very useful skill.

One, two, three days go by in silence. There are conventions. Even if you never intend to see the person again, you expect a phone call at least, a note, a bunch of flowers: it was nice, how are you? I was thinking about you. That intimacy, that degree of intimacy, even if it means nothing, it always means something. Or am I being old fashioned. Am I becoming middle aged?! God forbid!

Eventually you can't wait anymore. You phone him at the office.
He's on another call, can I help?
You ask her to have him call you back.
A moment later the telephone rings.

Hello, he says, his voice bobs and weaves like a bunch of balloons.
Oh hello, you say breezily, what I was ringing you about was . . .
Hey, wait a minute, I rang you.
But I just rang and left a message for you to ring back.
Well I didn't get it. I just had the urge to speak to you so I picked up the phone. Isn't that strange? He muses: synchronicity.
Sure, you say and continue your sentence: the reason I was ringing was . . .
You don't believe me, do you?

You'd like to. But he's right, you don't. You realize that you don't believe anything a man says: it's black, it's white, it's raining out, the world is round and Madrid is the capital of the moon . . . You're always looking for evidence to substantiate their claims.

'It doesn't matter,' you reply and continue to the end of your carefully rehearsed speech.

I've been here before.

You read me a poem over the telephone. About secretaries sucking off their bosses. I've heard it, I've seen it. Are there really so few scenes, so few stories, so few plots? Perhaps you got it from a film we both saw, a novel we both read before we met.

I've just found this poem for you, he says, and proceeds to read it . . .

What does it mean? Am I the secretary? Are you the boss? But you don't pose the question. Like lying about your age, or moving down the carriage in the underground. Fear: you mustn't admit the possibility.

And the second night he leaves his dressing gown: red with black polka-dots, silk. (Yes, there is a braided cord.) Not a deliberate act, you decide, this leaving behind, but still it means something. This is the problem when everything is a metaphor, everything means something other than it's meant to mean. The trick is in the interpretation.

It's only after he's gone that you discover the dressing gown, like the letter that arrives after the corpse has been interred. After he's made you breakfast and kissed you goodbye: 'This is the first minute of the rest of your life . . .' or 'I'll call you . . .' or 'Be good . . .' or 'Take care . . .' or 'Don't do anything I wouldn't do . . .', closing the front door softly behind him. It's only later that you discover it, tossed in a ball on the bathroom floor, under the bed, behind the sofa, waiting there for you to discover it long after he's returned to his faithfully waiting slippers and dog.

Dog. He likes dogs. He likes children and dogs. Doesn't this speak well of him?

I've heard this story before, how you drove the highway one cold winter night from Pittsburgh to Trois Rivières. The sickening thud. The dog whimpering, writhing – was it a bitch or is that my projection?
You walking the long dark road to the farmhouse to borrow a gun.
How she didn't die the first time. How she looked at you – those eyes – as you pulled the trigger. Once. Again.

Then the long walk back again for a spade.
Then the third walk back to return it.
The longest night, you say. And am I supposed to admire
– what? Your integrity?
And why do you tell me this story again and again?

And what about your wife, where is she? At the bottom of the hole, sucking and sucking for all her life, gasping for air at the bottom of this tunnel we're sliding down.
Listen. I can hear her. Listen. She is gasping, desperate, she is sucking up her life.

And so the calls begin. Friday night, the red eye blinking urgently.

Saturday, you cut the party early, hurry home and there it is again.

Sunday, you stay in all day to silence, on the off-chance.
Finally at six you pop out for a pint of milk and at your return there it is, the red eye winking wickedly: 'It's me.
Another unsuccessful attempt to contact you. It doesn't matter . . .'
(Doesn't it?)
So you put in another sleepless night.

Hello? Can I speak to . . . Yes, I will hold . . . Hello?
Look you've got to help me on this, I haven't been a mistress/girlfriend/bit on the side/adultress – no, I'm not the married one this time, it's you who's the adulterer.
I'm simply the Other Woman . . .
(Is this progress? I ask myself.)

Tell me, which is more acceptable? To ring you at home or at work?

You can call me as late as you like, you said once, but you didn't give me a number.

It's midnight, you say on the message, I'm still awake, you can ring as late as you like.

(But how late is that? But what is your telephone number?)

It's two o'clock in the morning. I have just come in and your message invites me to ring. Any time. But surely, however quickly you jump on the phone – I don't sleep at night anyway, you've said, I sleep with the phone right beside my bed.

But surely, however quickly you grab it, the noise will echo through the house, maybe not actually waking your wife if she does indeed sleep deep, though I doubt that she sleeps as deeply as you claim . . .

But still the ring would work its way in, careening madly through her dreams like the distant tolling of the bell in the pastoral scene which suddenly screams into the morning wake-up alarm. Like the cry which at first you absorb and integrate into the story: birdsong or a cow lowing in the pasture, which suddenly becomes a telephone or worse. When you wake with a start and think: how long has this been going on? It's the baby screaming in terror. For how long have I been lying here asleep while he/she/it was being tortured, tormented?

This is the moment when the gap opens, the yawning possibility asserts itself: somebody could be dying, someone could have died, crying in the night while you slept on, absorbing, denying the cries.

How long has this been going on?

And you didn't even wake.

So, what did you want to say? he says.
To say? About what?
You telephoned me.

Oh yes, oh just to say I have the tickets for Friday night. Are you still free?
Of course. What are we going to see?
An Enema of the People, by Henry K Gibson.
Fine, it's one of my favourites. I'll meet you there. Shall I drive or will you? It would be silly to have two cars.

. . . And so, once again, the illicit becomes mundane.

Does one ever learn?
Does one just keep making the same mistakes, over and over until one gives up from sheer exhaustion?

How often am I likely to see you? she asks one evening. If this continues, of course, she adds: don't startle the wild beast, don't challenge him with presumptions.
Weekly? he replies. It's a question, not a statement.
How far can you go? How little can you give? How much can you get away with? She doesn't reply. She's processing the information. It sticks like a snowball in her throat. It takes a few minutes to dissolve, to melt and trickle into the scalding pit of her gut.

I was driving along; the highway was busy. I saw a sign down the road for Highway 18, no, Highway 8 – I forget the number – the number isn't important; what I saw was the highway I needed. It was dusk so everything was difficult to see – the context, the surroundings. And I was in the wrong lane, but I managed to ease into the proper lane for the turn.

As soon as I got on the other highway the quality of the road diminished. Suddenly it was smaller – two lanes, not four – but there wasn't so much traffic so it was still OK, it didn't really matter.

I was driving now in the country, no more neon. It was barren, prairie perhaps, flat-topped mountains, long stretches of flat land between them, no water anywhere, no rivers, and this huge, enormous sky overhead, like a blanket, like an umbrella.

Suddenly the road in front started rearing up at me. I was going so fast, too fast, but I couldn't slow down. Calm, I thought, stay calm, but it seemed to go faster and faster, the car. I couldn't find the brakes. Eventually I found them, but they didn't work; the pedal just slammed right down to the floor with no resistance, no effect.

The thing is to concentrate. Keep control. Grip the steering wheel. Every gesture must be minute. Each fraction of a turn is magnified into a gut-churning veer. Just keep your grip. Anticipate. Concentrate. Eventually, if you can hold out long enough, the car will run out of gas. . . .

When I woke up I remembered the simulated racing car module on Brighton Pier, the one we had played on the week before. He'd climbed on first and reached a score of – I don't know, not quite enough to qualify.

The thing is though, after he crashed the first time the lights and noises flashed, then he got a second chance. But when I paid my 30p and climbed in, I crashed almost immediately because he had left it in high gear. He had left it in high gear without telling me. I waited for the game to start again, but it didn't. Game Over flashed up on the screen. I only got one chance.

But but . . . Even he admitted he thought I should have got a second try. No value for money anymore, he scowled, kicking the module as the man in the ticket booth shouted at us to get out of his amusement arcade.

Later, driving home that night, his hand on my thigh, he said: every time your foot hits the clutch I can feel the muscles tighten all up your leg. Yes . . . And . . .

As we pulled up in front of my flat he said: you drive very well.
What do you mean?
No nonsense, no drama, you just get in and do it.

My bed is a sea, tossed with whitecaps. My duvet cover, white on white, embroidered by squinting women in the underground cellars in Taiwan. My duvet is a snowbank from which I construct snowmen, build them up to knock them down: one kick and they crumble into feathers, contained in the white pool of my bed.

Why are you sad? he asks one night in the shadow of the streetlamp outside.
It's a shame one has to sleep with somebody just to get to know them.
You didn't have to sleep with me, did you? We could have done it slowly over cups of coffee in cafés.
You'd never have spared me the time.

He reflects. He doesn't deny. He rests his hand on the curve of my belly and slowly slips into sleep.

I don't want to be made a fool of.
You're too clever to be made a fool of.
Nobody's too clever to be made a fool of.

Sometimes in the darkness she drew his arms around her like a scarf. Sometimes she threw them off. Sometimes she curled herself into the curve of his belly like the heart of an artichoke, the soft leaves, the succulent part which the connoisseurs crave, hacking away, discarding the bitter, tough, outer armour, probing for the sweet salty bits, the lick of leaf, the quiver, the shiver which can expand to an earthquake and explode.

Sometimes she threw herself across him, joined at the belly, an octopus of arms and legs, a tangle of limbs thrown heavy, carelessly discarded, cast outwards into the four corners of the bed. A hand, an elbow, a calf, a wrist: is this hers or his? Does it matter. All that signifies is the weight of limb bearing down on limb.

I have been dreaming about him again, dreams I can't recall at dawn.

The marks which we make, flesh on flesh, which
disappear – or seem to – each time a body moves.

Why are you sad?
This isn't what I want. I'm not looking for a casual acquaintance; I'm looking for a partner. And you're not available.
I'm here, aren't I?
For tonight, not forever.
Nothing is forever.

(. . . 'And you always hope that this will be the one that breaks the pattern . . .')

This control. This discipline. I don't think I can handle it. I'm the sort that wants to grab it by the neck and nail it down and suck the life out of it and label it and turn the page.

You have to slow down driving into the turn, speed up coming out of it.
Don't rush your fences.

Careful, you might have blood on you.
I didn't notice any.
I hope nobody else does.
It's not likely.

What do you want from this? she asks; what did you expect to get?
Conversation. Intimacy. It isn't the sex which I miss, it's the waking up, it's the body next to you in the bed when you wake up at night; that's what I miss.

Intimacy. This intimacy begins and ends with the skin.

Are you in love with him?

R used to say the only man you'll really love is your husband, because he's the only man who ever left you. Perhaps I really do love this man, certainly he never will be mine.

The man beside the water, urging: step in, go on, step in, little girl, the river will wash it away.

I must keep reminding myself it isn't you that I want, it's just somebody.
Why don't you want me?
Because you're not available.
I'm here as long as you want me.
Here, now, this moment. But a moment doesn't last.

For Christ's sake this is ridiculous; we're not even playing in the same ball park. I'm looking for a full-time long-term companion, you don't want any more than a once-a-week casual fuck.
I didn't realize this was a game, he muses.
Of course it's a game; don't be ingenuous.

Dearest . . .
No, not dearest . . .
Dear . . . No.
Hi? Too casual.
Begin with no salutation. Simply begin:
I'm missing you.
No: thinking of you. Bad move to admit it, I know, but I always was pretty reckless at games . . .

Don't sleep.
Don't go to sleep on me, please.
But he does. Breathing like a forest.
How to distinguish the wood from the trees.

You watch his eyes, flickering shadows over the bleak terrain of his face.
You will him to wake. Talk to me, please. Don't leave me like this, don't desert me, don't abandon me in this dark night.
But he does.

You whisper his name, you watch to make sure that the rhythm of his breathing doesn't alter. You hazard it, softly:
I love you, you whisper into his dream.

No response.

You decide it is safe;

You love me, you whisper.
You do. Don't you? You do. You love me.
You slip the words into his dream like a pin in the ear.

Say something often enough it becomes true.

Do you even want this man? Probably not. Probably you only want to know you have him so you can reject him. Like all the others. Toss him back. Flickering, gasping, quivering, into the oily, black waters.

The harlequin, the bulls, the clowns, the misfits, '*el loco*', appear early in Picasso's work. The ladies of loose morals, the divan, the women with children begging in doorways. Please, Picasso, notice me; but he doesn't so she starves, unmarked while he continues designing menus for 'El Quatre Gats': a lady with a dog at her feet. Is this a sense of humour? she asks, as the life ebbs away from her down the walls of the castle, down the terra cotta of the hilltop, though the tree line into the sea. Is it enough to be a great man's muse? A muse. Amuse. Am used.

The 1902 sketch of Picasso sitting, dressed in his large overcoat, beside a nude whose face is turned away on the bed. Woman about to be abandoned: a vase of pretty flowers downstage, a woman about to be abandoned, immortalized of course, but abandoned nonetheless.

The subjects came early, recurring through his life: the artist and his muse, or perhaps one should call it the courtesan and her a-musement . . .

It's the growing ease, the knowing how to let go, let the subject paint itself. The bowl of fruit, the violin, the sleeping lady. 'The true artist puts everything he/she knows into each piece of work.'

'It reads as though she fears she'll never speak again, as though she's thrown in everything she knows just in case this is her only chance.' This is what they'll say. And what about my recipe for marmalade, or strawberry jam – not the sort that's made on the roofs in Marrakesh, but normal, homemade strawberry jam from wild berries hand-picked in the fields of Vermont: *verts monts*.

The strawberry is the symbol of good works; it represents the righteous, whose labours are the fruits of the spirit.

You see, there's a lot I haven't told you yet. Like who has had the abortions and who has had the affairs, and who has attempted suicide and who has submitted to blackmail and who has courted oblivion in all the other ways.

The problem is, people read the story and think they know you intimately; they think it is all true.

Paint yourself into the picture, you always do.
Every portrait is a self-portrait: '*Madame Bovary, c'est moi.*'
Velazquez lounges discreetly in the doorway as the posers primp and preen, feigning ignorance of the camera, acting spontaneous. And the dog in the foreground hovers, unaware that he is more metaphor, more emblem or icon than living, breathing flesh. Not knowing, not caring.

The spider's webs, the hieroglyphs my sheets make on his body. How to interpret them?

My lover arrives at midnight. He sleeps like a tree, he sighs like a jungle all night long, one large warm paw

placed gently on my back, belly, thigh, adjusting as I thrash and flail. For such a tormented person he sleeps with an enviable ease.
What makes you think I'm tormented?
Nobody covers as much ground as you do who isn't being pursued.

You lie on the sofa. Four o'clock in the morning, wrapped in an old blanket, waiting for your lover who was due one, two, three hours ago. The tape plays Mozart's clarinet concerto. The sad, central movement reminds you of a friend who died last year – no, two years ago. He wasn't even a very close friend, but now that he's gone you long to see him. You talk to him often in your head: what would you do in this situation? What do you think about x or y?

The candle flickers. The cars pass. So many travellers so late at night and each one makes you seize up with anticipation. But they speed up as they approach. Then the long slow sigh as they recede into the distant dawn. And still you lie here waiting.

This is your life! You must inhabit it! This isn't a story or a painting or a still from some moving picture. This is all there is and it's passing like the traffic which never stops outside your door. But still it's hard to concentrate on anything except the lover for whom you lie here waiting.

Let's get this straight once and for all.
I am not imploring you to come.
I'm simply asking if you will be there,
that's all.

And finally they arrive, the words, the lines you have been dreading, have been longing for like the lights of the oncoming traffic, like the water swirling round your ears. You made me feel young, he says.

(The line slips easy –
a flat stone skipped into the sea:
he has practised this act,
perfected it . . . Almost.)

Funny – you make me feel very old.

And your heart contracts till it's small and hard like a bullet lodged in your chest, waiting to explode.

And in the end, when it's over, he says, as you knew he would, as you begged him not to say at the very beginning, on the very first day, he casts his eyes down to the ground and says it:
I'm sorry.
That's all. I'm sorry.
That's it.

Shall I return to M? He is the centre of my alphabet.
Or R? He is still out there, waiting, somewhere.

You can only leave a man so many times before it all becomes ridiculous.

This too will heal, someday, if I can only stop picking at the scab. The wound will close over, leaving . . . what? An almost infinitesimal scar. Invisible to everyone but me.

Perhaps we should tattoo ourselves, carve our passions in our cheeks, thighs, the palms of our hands. Initiation rites. Perhaps we should display our scars like war medals. Perhaps we should stain the anemones with blood so nobody can forget or deny what has passed between us.

I should have said . . .
I should have said . . .
I should . . .

27 The Thames

Never go backwards in life, my grandmother said. The one piece of advice I remember. Contemplating the move from Hampstead down to Camden Town. The litter. The dirt. The black profile of your face on the white towel when you wash in the evening. I hate the thought of moving. The thought of leaving once again.

Moving moving moving again. Moving on. The prospect of the downward slide, the hollow in the foothills, the soft swamp land with its permanent halo of dirt hovering; always tentative, never lifting, criss-crossed overhead by railroad tracks: the Northern line, the slowest, oldest, frailest line, the deepest line in London. And it bisects the horizon of my new garden.

Never go backwards in life, Anna repeats. I contemplate – no, confront – the slowly slipping path. This coming down from the height of the Heath to the village in the foothills.

Well it looks rather quaint, rather French with all the overhead railway lines, with the bus depot at the end of the road, with the pubs spilling over the sidewalks onto the street. At least it has street credibility, she smiles wanly, smiles faintly with sisterly compassion. Well at least no one can say that this is twee, she consoles.

Houses are so emotional; these issues – moving houses, where one lives – they matter so much more to women, don't you think? she mutters. Try not to be so emotional.

I am sliding downhill like the river. I am slipping down into the Thames. The Effra, the Falcon, the Fleet, the

Graveney, the Quaggy, the Tyburn, the Walbrook, the Wandle.

It's the rise I love. It's the rise that hits at the base of the hill, at the end of the plateau of the High Street with its endless parade of dinky shops, when the hill begins to mount up ahead and you climb through Chalk Farm and Belsize Park and into Hampstead past the Heath right up to the pond: 'Highest point in central London.' And the Post Office Tower and the dome of St Paul's and the lego lights of Centre Point and the black silk ribbon of the river snaking through the city and the sequinned skirts of South London beyond, and beyond that the Channel, then Calais, Paris, Toulouse, Marseilles, the Blue Train to the Riviera. And Istanbul and Marrakesh beyond. And Rio de Janeiro.

I always try to live at the top of the house at the top of the street at the top of the hill looking down on the world, I tried to explain, but she wasn't impressed. A bird in a gilded cage swinging crazily on the thinnest branches at the top of the tallest tree. This is the way the Fleet runs, from the heights of the Heath, underground to the heart of the city.

Dearest J: I hate to move again.

Dearest J: please find my newest change of address. I wish you'd seen the last place. And the place before that. I'll send you a photo.

Dearest J: the divorce came through this morning. Two years' separation more or less. Just plop. Just like that: a simple brown envelope on the floor with all the other circulars and fliers, bills and requests and notes and messages – junk male. The decree absolute. So now we are no longer one.

Up and down.
Back and forth.
In and out.

Down into the city, up onto the Heath.
Down to the river bottom, up to the surface for air.
Back and forth across the city, the continent, the ocean.

In and out: the beast with two backs/with one back/with a vibrator/a blanket/a hot cup of cocoa in front of the TV.

What does it mean? What does it amount to?

I'm feeling rather miserable this morning. Tomorrow is my birthday. The swallows shat all over my car again last night. I must remember to stop parking it under the telephone lines.

Dearest J: I'm thirty-three years old. This is the middle of my life. I'm almost halfway through my three score and ten. And what do I have to show for it? A catalogue of names and places. This is the man I lived with then, this is the place we lived in. This is the place I lived in alone. This is the man I travelled with to London and Paris, to Rio and Rome and Mombasa and Marrakesh.

No I have never travelled on my own.
No I have never not been alone.

Sometimes I forget the names. Sometimes I try to count them: M I will always remember, he was my thirteenth lover. A was my first. And each one I leave I am sure will be my last but they just keep on coming: bullets from a machine gun, ninepins in a bowling lane.

The Effra, the Falcon, the Fleet, the Graveney, the Quaggy, the Tyburn, the Walbrook, the Wandle. The Thames. The Channel: *la Manche*. The Ocean.

I will never forget the man who took me to the river. I will never find the dog that passed on the other side of the water. Not that particular and unique spotted dog. Though there may be – almost certainly there will be – other dogs and men.